A
BOOK
OF
TRICKS

Emma Cooke (1934 –) was born in Portarlington, Co. Laois and was educated at Alexandra College, Dublin. Her short stories began to appear in the Irish Press's New Irish Writing page in 1971, at which time she, her husband and nine children were living in Limerick. She now lives in Killaloe, Co. Clare and resident children have been replaced by visiting grandchildren.

In recent years she has worked as Writer in Residence for Tipperary N.R. County Council (2001-2002) and with Kerry County Council (2003-2004). *A Book of Tricks* is her fourth novel and began as a short story published in an anthology she edited and produced for Tipperary N.R. Arts Office.

Emma is also the author of numerous articles, stories for radio, and has taught creative writing classes under the Writers in Schools, and the Writers in Prisons' schemes as well as for various adult education programmes. She is also an enthusiastic *haiku* writer and has recently produced a collection entitled *The Mermaid's Purse* (Published by Kerry Co. Council & the Arts Council, January 2004) of haiku written by herself and fellow enthusiasts, young and old, she met during her stay in Kerry.

PUBLISHED WORK

Female Forms
short stories 1988

A Single Sensation
novel 1981

Eve's Apple
novel 1985

Wedlocked
novel 1994

A BOOK OF TRICKS

EMMA COOKE

Wynkin
deWorde

2004

Published in 2004
by

**Wynkin
deWorde**

Wynkin deWorde Ltd.,
PO Box 257, Galway, Ireland.
info@deworde.com

A CIP catalogue record for this book is available from the British Library

ISBN: 1-904893-01-5

Typeset by Patricia Hope, Skerries, Co. Dublin, Ireland
Cover Illustration by Roger Derham
Cover Design Supervision: Design Direct, Galway, Ireland
Printed by Betaprint, Dublin, Ireland

ACKNOWLEDGEMENTS

To Roger Derham, Brenda Derham and Valerie Shortland of
Wynkin de Worde for their advice, generous encouragement and
attention to detail.

To Melanie Scott, Arts Officer with Tipperary N. County
Council, who gave a sympathetic ear to the opening chapters,
and Kate Kennelly, Arts Officer with Kerry County Council,
and Kathleen Browne, Kerry County Librarian, who saw me to
the finishing line.

Also, I would like to mention a series of talks on the tarot
given by Father Mark Patrick Hederman of Glenstal Abbey in
the spring of 2002. They suggested fresh ways of approaching a
manuscript and opened up new possibilities.

Finally, love and gratitude to my six lovely daughters and
three stalwart sons who are always there for me.

DEDICATION

Dedicated to my grandchildren:
Geoffrey, Rachael, Emily, Diarmuid, Ailbhe, Kevin,
Brendan, Niall, Heather, John, Caroline, Jennifer, Alison,
Emma, Tara, J.J., Conor, Jessica, Jonathan, Jack,
Philip, Olivia and Louis.

INDIAN ROPE TRICK

From the very beginning I expected my mother to climb back down from wherever she'd hidden herself. As soon as I could write I wrote her letters begging her to come back. "I hate my Auntie Theo," was how I began. I told her how scared I was when Auntie Theo came at me with her wooden spoon. Auntie Theo was a very angry person. It was because she was so holy, although she was not a Roman Catholic like we children and Daddy were.

I described my new bicycle. I asked her to come home for Christmas. I asked her if she thought my red dress was prettier than my green one.

I wrote her a poem:

> *Her mother wept and called her Dad.*
> *The blood poured from the girl's deep wound,*
> *They could not save her, they were sad.*

I wrote and asked her to make the wooden spoon vanish. I wrote that Daddy had been home for the weekend and I'd beaten him at draughts. I never mentioned his friend, Myrna, whose hotel he stayed in most of the time in Dublin if he wasn't travelling to Europe or England on business. The most we saw of

1

him was a day or two during the week. I did tell her about Beth Page, my best friend who was four days older than I was. I wrote that Mrs Page missed her and cried the time I asked her about the rope trick and people vanishing and never coming back.

In spite of my pleas my mother never did return, although sometimes the Madonna picture on the upstairs landing that moved and smiled seemed to be conveying a loving message from her.

I had two sisters, Alice and Lynda, but they were much older. Alice was 22 and Lynda 20. Even my brother Josh, the closest to me in age, was eighteen. I was twelve years old. An afterthought, according to Auntie Theo. A bundle of trouble. A nuisance.

The big ones refused to talk to me about the rope trick.

"Just shut up, Fran. You know she's dead," Alice said, slapping down the cards on the red shiny formica top of the kitchen table. We were starting a game of 45. Lynda puckered her lips as she doused a tea bag into a blue mug of hot water. She was the family beauty with heavy blonde hair that fell in thick coils over her shoulders. Alice was like me, thin, dark and nervy. Josh was the boy. Pimples, an earring, curls, a beard that wouldn't grow. It was the late 1980s.

I couldn't let myself believe that Mummy was dead. That meant Auntie Theo would be in charge of us forever. She'd been running the household for as long as I could remember and she was ruining my life. I threw my cards into the centre of the table and walked away while Josh, who was my partner, howled at me to come back.

There were no ropes in our house anywhere. None in the outhouses, or the greenhouse, or in the boot of Daddy's Mercedes. I knew because once his car wouldn't start and Mr Page came round to give him a tow and said, "What we need is a piece of rope."

Daddy immediately smacked his forehead and walked in a circle round the fountain saying, "Christ's Sake, Nat, there are no ropes in this house. None. Do you hear me? None." And Mr Page said, "Easy on there Henry. Of course there aren't. It's alright old son. I should have brought one with me. We'll manage something. Poor Jane. Oh Jesus, I could cut my tongue out!"

As always my ears pricked up when my mother's name was mentioned, but they went straight from there into talking about the insides of cars.

Round in Page's house Beth and I often climbed ropes. There was a big outhouse with a loft at the very end of their long narrow garden. We'd start by catching the rope in both hands in front of our faces. Then we'd fix it between the sole of our right foot and the top of our left. Next: ready, steady go – bottom hand over the top hand and our insteps gripping further up each time. Beth first because it was her loft, me beneath her thinking we'll soon be there, we'll soon be there.

We were very fond of the loft. It smelt of apples and damp. Some of the slates were missing and we could sit with saucers of strawberries on our laps, staring at the clouds through the gaps. Fine wisps of gauze, small pieces of fluff that were easy to draw, ones that screened passing aeroplanes so that it seemed the sky itself was rumbling, long flattish-looking ones onto which a person could climb from the top of a rope if it reached up high enough and sit comfortably until big anvil-headed clouds came and chopped them to pieces – storm clouds which were heavy grey lumps that bumped into each other and made tears spill from the sky and form into pools on the loft's rotting floor.

Someday, someday I'd make the journey up there myself and I'd find Mummy and bring her back. I knew exactly how she looked, although there were no photographs of her, not even in Auntie Theo's bedroom. She was very like the Madonna in our picture – kind, with gentle eyes. I was only an infant when she disappeared, but sometimes she showed up in my dreams and she always looked the same.

The nicest thing was that when you got up beyond the clouds you were in a land of eternal sunshine.

On the level beneath the loft, life was rude. Once we peeped down through the trapdoor and had to hold our noses to keep from giggling aloud because Mr Page came in and took a quick piss against the wall. If he'd discovered us the loft would have been sealed off and we'd have lost our den. Even though it was in danger of falling down, with holes in the floor as well as the roof, it was our very favourite place. We did all sorts of things there. Once, when Mrs Page refused to let Beth keep a hamster in the house because Beth's grandmother, who lived with them, wouldn't believe it wasn't a rat even when Beth carried it over to her snuggled comfortably on the palm of her hand, we kept it hidden in the loft until it died during a cold spell in wintertime and had to be buried beside the rhubarb patch.

INDIAN ROPE TRICK

Jane's father was born in India. His father worked for the Indian Civil Service. My father-in-law had once seen a man shin up a rope faster than a monkey and disappear into thin air. As well as the vanishing man he'd seen elephants with solid gold howdahs transporting Highnesses, rubies and emeralds as big as fists hanging round their necks. He'd seen armless beggars who could wind their legs around their waists, magicians who could make a tree grow from a seed, and a chicken hatch out of an egg in a split-second. And snake charmers, of course, lots of snake charmers. None of this impressed my family who refused to have anything to do with me after I'd married Jane.

It wasn't because of her father's exotic memories, but because of my people's folk memory of her paternal great-grandfather. Old Smyth Drummond had evicted my ancestors from their miserable dwellings in East Clare and forced them to trudge the long road from Bodyke to County Tipperary, their pathetic bundles clutched tight to their scrawny chests. If I married a daughter of the house of Smyth Drummond I was as bad as any informer, or traitor, or turncoat in our whole terrible history. Jane's people were notorious for their plundering ways and their bad blood. Not to mention their horsey accents and their allegiance to the British Empire and all its evil ways. The Smyth Drummonds had taken in British officers during the Civil War. How dare I, Henry Cleeve, bring shame upon my father's memory.

"It was our pride saw us through," my mother said. "That and our Catholic faith." Her family hadn't been evicted. She was a Tipperary person back as far as could be traced. "Thank God your grandfather didn't live to see this day," she said reminding me of his years in jail, his total loyalty to the Big Fellow and the portrait of Patrick Pearse in profile in our sitting-room alongside President John F Kennedy and Pope John XXIII. My father was already dying slowly of cancer and had no energy to argue one way or the other.

Smyth Drummond's big house and land were gone long before Jane was born. When we met it was nothing but a blackened shell with trees growing through the gaps in the walls but that made no difference to my family. Jane's father had been, of all things, a Protestant clergyman. She and her sister, Theo grew up in a huge, freezing midland rectory with mice scampering behind the wainscoting and rain leaking through the gammy roof onto their beds in bad weather.

We fell in love instantly. She even fell in love with my religion and claimed her late father had always admired the faith of the people. At the time we met she was living with her mother and her sister in a gloomy rented flat in a basement in Blackrock, County Dublin. I was a qualified engineer about to set up my own practice in Limerick city. It was 1965 and Ireland was on the up and up, with the sky the limit.

If I'd known how it would end I'd have run a mile. How do you tell your kids their mother has hanged herself?

You don't. You make up stories. You tell them that she wasn't well and God took her away. You tell them that they mustn't be sad because she's in a happy place. You have "Fallen asleep" inscribed on her tombstone – although, that's not at all how she looked.

I covered my face with my hands to shut out the horror while the guards said: "Sir, we're very sorry about this sir, but it has to be done." They were so embarrassed that they'd taken their hats off in respect.

Afterwards I had the old coach house where she hanged herself from a rafter pulled to the ground and built two town houses that I sold immediately for a handsome profit. In those days, even when the worst happened, I had the Midas touch. The way I was headed I'd end up festooned with emeralds and rubies like a Maharajah myself.

When Jane died I urgently needed someone to look after the kids. We did have live-in help, but she was lazy and hopeless. Besides, she started complaining that she was afraid the place was haunted. She felt nervous whenever she was the only adult in the house. She needed company – although Winnie Page told me that she had company. Her boyfriend moved in during the night hours whenever I wasn't there.

In spite of the awful tragedy my business continued to expand. I was opening an office in Dublin as well as continuing with the Limerick one and had to be away from home several nights a week. I was at my wit's end. When Jane's ailing mother died within weeks of Jane's suicide, her going expedited by shame and grief, Theo announced that for poor Jane's sake she'd move down to Riverview for the time being and run the household until I'd made proper plans. I was so grateful that I made her a present of the pearls I'd given Jane when Fran was born. I told myself that the children needed someone to keep a constant eye on them. They were becoming as wild as young goats. I didn't even mind if she gave out hell to them from time to time, or administered an occasional wallop. It was probably what they needed.

As Theo moved in I gradually moved out. I spent more time away than in Limerick. When I did come home Theo discreetly disappeared and left the children to me. She belonged to various bible study groups and other churchy organizations. The house was clean, everyone's faces washed, onions hung from ceiling hooks in the kitchen, herbs grew on the window sill, there was a cooked chicken or casserole waiting to be eaten. The baby, Fran, turned into a toddler, then a little girl, then a little girl with a schoolbag, then a girl who was nearly up to my shoulder, then a gangling twelve year old with a heartbreaking gap between her two front teeth and a grin that reminded me so much of Jane it hurt to look at her.

In Dublin during the first two years after Jane's death I did some stupid things, slept with some women I'd rather forget about, and generally behaved like a zombie except on the business front. However once I'd found Myrna's place – a small hotel off Leeson Street with a pretty proprietress and odd opening hours it quickly became my refuge. Apart from the obvious attractions it was a good contact place. Country politicians, visiting architects, race-horse owners, entrepreneurs, spin doctors, media people, builders home from England and other people who would happily mark your card for you in return for some free professional advice were all frequent guests.

My affair with Myrna was conducted discreetly, mostly during afternoon siestas when I slipped out of the Baggot Street office for an hour or two. The nights were given over to drinking sessions that carried on into the small hours, followed by a blissful stint of anaesthetised sleep.

I never talked to her about Jane. One late lunchtime when there was only myself at the counter eating roast lamb and Myrna behind it with her hands submerged in the small stainless sink peeling onions under water she asked, out of the blue, "Whatever happened to your wife, Henry?"

"She died," I said.

"How?"

"Suddenly."

The lamb had wedged itself in my chest.

"Poor you," she gave me a deep look. Then she put the sliced onions onto a plate, pulled the plug out of the sink and said, "If you peel them under water you don't cry."

She was wearing a wine-coloured low-necked sweater that accentuated her voluptuous breasts. I eyed them and thought of suggesting we go upstairs for a while but the entrance door burst open and two American women with happy-day smiles and armloads of parcels waddled in looking for cups of good strong coffee.

The other important influence in my life was Nat Page. I'd known him since my schooldays. We'd gone to the same boarding school in Ennis. I was there because an uncle of my mother's was its president. Nat had been sent by a moneyed aunt who wanted him to have a good education. Although we were friends I never knew many details of his background. He was a person who lived totally for the present and the future.

It seemed a happy coincidence that we'd both settled in Limerick at the same time. He'd married a local big shot's daughter and been designated heir to the big shot's accountancy firm. Winnie was a lovely person. Plump, freckled, with honest grey eyes that followed Nat's every move with adoration. I only hoped that she'd never find out about his womanising. Even allowing for adolescent bragging, it had been legendary since fifth class when he'd managed to score at least twice on even a modest school outing to the Burren and environs, or Dublin's National Museum.

From the time of our reunion in Limerick he was better than a brother to me. His father-in-law had died a few months earlier and Nat was running the business. He and Winnie had moved into the large redbrick house on the Ennis Road where the only fly in the ointment was Winnie's mother, a formidable Limerick matron with a penchant for large hats, and larger amounts of gin and tonic. They had no children as yet, but Nat wasn't worried.

There are some people who play such a vital part in your story that you can't remember life without them. That's the way it was with Nat. He walked into my office just after I'd opened it, reintroduced himself, and right away took charge of all my financial affairs. When I began to make money he put it where it would make the most interest. He handled my outgoings and incomings. He dealt with the Revenue vultures and set up my bank accounts.

"You'll be a bloody millionaire before you're 60. You can retire then, Henry. Relax, enjoy."

He planned to do the same thing himself. He painted pictures of sultry dark-eyed women with no knickers, ourselves turned into a pair of satyrs, no snakes in the grass to spoil our fun. "No in-laws," he'd say. Sometimes in the small hours in the Rowing Club bar he'd paint vivid pictures of the tortures he'd inflict on Winnie's mother, Mrs Quill, if he could have her stretched out on a rack.

After Jane died he stopped feeding me these flights of fancy and simply did the best he could for me. He knew all the tricks. He was a man of the world.

A BALL OF STRING

Beth and I had gone on a camping trip with the girl guides up on the shores of Lough Derg. I was worried because I'd just started my first period. I'd spent ages studying the instructions on the packet of tampons that Alice gave me when I told her, but I was still afraid, no matter what she said, that it was going to slip right up into my stomach. I'd even got a pain in my tummy as if it had happened already. Alice had said a pain in your tummy was a natural part of the curse inflicted on women and to take no notice of it.

When it got late we sat around the campfire telling stories. After a while we did some tricks. Chinese burns, three card tricks, making people say "No", making pennies disappear. I showed everyone how to tie a knot while holding both ends of a piece of twine. After that we sat for a while in the smoky dusk watching the fire crackle and hiss.

Then Beth told us about a man who could swallow a whole ball of twine, make a nick in his stomach just over his belly button, push out an inch of the cord and let someone else take hold of it and keep pulling.

"It was some sort of fake."

"No it wasn't."

"It'd be all bloody."

"It was."

"From his stomach?"

"Jeez – it'd be worse than having a baby."

"Or period pains," I said.

"Stop showing off Fran," Beth said. She was annoyed because she was as flat as a washboard and had no sign of any big girl stuff yet. She hadn't even got pubic hair which made her embarrassed when we went swimming.

"I saw it on television," Beth said. "It was like a horrible red worm coming out inch by inch.

We put our hands over our ears before she could tell us any more. Then we told some ghost stories, and ones about the pookah, and fairies that carried away healthy babies and left sickly ones in their place. After a while our leader went down to look at the effect of moonlight on the lake water and we began to play truth or dare.

Another reason Beth was angry was because the head nun had picked me to be a prefect but had made the mistake of not choosing her as well. When a cruel girl with lank hair and a funny smell held up the string I'd used for my trick and said, "I dare you to swallow this Fran, or else." she backed her up enthusiastically.

I shook my head and tried to laugh it off, but it didn't work.

"Come on. Come on. It's only a short piece."

"I'd practically choke myself in the first minute," I said.

"You eat spaghetti."

Beth had taken a cigarette from the packet she'd filched from Mrs Page's purse and was sharing it with the lank-haired girl.

"Cowardy custard," she grinned at me. "It's not even poisonous."

"Then you'll have to tell us the truth," the cruel girl said. "What happened to your mother?"

She twisted the length of twine round her skinny fingers.

"My mother lives abroad," I said. "Daddy and I are going out to visit her in the summer. She's delicate. The climate here is too damp. She has a rare heart disease."

"Liar," the girl said. "Tell the truth, or else."

"Give me that," I snatched the piece of string from her. I had to save my sad, tragic mother from her sneering curiosity.

"Swallow it now, no cheating," Beth said.

"That's what I'm going to do," I said. "And if I die it will be your fault."

The string felt fat against my palate as I tilted my head back and, trying not to gag, let it slip towards my throat. The first gulp was the hardest, then I pushed my tongue up and made it press against the roof of my mouth and I felt the string move another fraction. It was like climbing a rope, except you were doing it inside out. I saw the twine wriggling down my gullet and its tip swinging in the red cavern of my belly. It wasn't spaghetti, it had turned into steel wire. My throat was beginning to close as I felt it pulling everything tight, like a drawstring. I batted my free hand to warn the others not to come near me. My eyes were closed. If someone stepped forward and caught the end of it now and tugged all my innards would come out in one quick jerk the way a chicken's did when the man in the poultry shop cleaned it. Then, shockingly, the twine had got itself tangled in my windpipe and it was going to strangle me. They were all going to be in trouble when I was dead. I couldn't cry out. I'd lost my voice. I felt like the time I went to Holy Communion and swallowed the host in a state of mortal sin, because I'd stolen money from Daddy's coat pocket. And now my throat was closing in, I'd have to gag. If I did I'd choke. I felt as if I had a rope around my neck instead of a piece of twine inside me. All you had to do to tie a knot in a piece of string while holding both ends was to cross your arms before you picked it up. It had been a silly trick to show them. I'd handed them the weapon for my own destruction. The string was pulling my head forward and my eyes had started to pop. I was afraid to do anything but keep swallowing even though it seemed to be getting larger and larger, wriggling up through my brain and down to the soles of my feet. I opened my eyes a fraction and saw my challenger staring at me with her mouth hanging open. She'd remember this for the rest of her life.

13

I'd come back and haunt her when she least expected it. This was it. Suddenly I didn't care anymore. I was even happy that I'd taken on the challenge. Daddy was going to be so upset. Everyone in the school was going to be so upset. My brother and sisters would sit around talking about me in soft voices. Auntie Theo would be filled with remorse. I was a saint. I couldn't have pulled the string back out even if I tried.

W-h-o-o-o-f-f-!

It was Beth who thumped me on the back and the others who caught me before I pitched forward into the fire.

I lay on my side on the bumpy damp grass smelling of sick and coughing and spluttering up my sausages and beans.

"What's happening here?" Our camp leader strode back from admiring the moonlight on the lake.

"Fran nearly choked," the guides chorused.

I lay there with the twine twisting round like a sea serpent in my belly.

The pain got worse when we were in our tent in our sleeping bags. I could feel the twine pressing against my belly button. I'd put in a fresh tampon, but it seemed to have wriggled its way up into my gut. I felt so bad that I had to wake Beth and tell her.

"You didn't swallow it, you spat it out when you threw up," she hissed.

"Where is it so?"

"Where do you think? Buried with your puke. It's your bloody period. Just keep quiet about it. There's nothing wrong with you. You only put the end of the string in your mouth."

I didn't believe her. She was making it up to keep me quiet. Later on I vomited again, all over my sleeping bag and the sweater I had on over my pyjamas.

Next morning the twine had solidified into one huge piece of gristle. It lay heavily on my stomach so that I couldn't eat breakfast, but just had a mug of tea. By the time we struck camp and headed home that evening it was still in the same place, right over my belly button. I asked Beth to feel it but she told me to stop being such a notice box. It was a Sunday afternoon and the day was still warm and sunny when we got back to Limerick. There was nobody about, so I put on my red swimsuit, unfolded a sunbed in the garden and lay down letting the warmth fall on my sore belly. Dusty, our family mongrel, kept me company. He came and begged for biscuits, and when he realised I hadn't any he licked my toes then collapsed onto the grass like a moth-eaten rug.

After a while I could feel the gristle melting and becoming more liquid so I had to go to the bathroom. One good thing was that I'd finished bleeding. The thought that this was going to happen every four weeks until I was an old lady was very depressing.

When I came back out again I fell fast asleep. I was woken by Auntie Theo shaking me and asking why I was lazing about when the drawing room, dining room, study and front room all needed to be polished and tidied. We'd had no household help for some years. Auntie Theo said it was a sinful waste to pay someone to clean up after strong healthy young people. I, being the youngest, was the one she picked on most when jobs needed to be done.

"I don't feel well," I pleaded.

She ignored my excuse. "When you have the rooms done there's the bath, and the shower room and the downstairs lavatory."

"It's Sunday," I said. Auntie Theo never broke the Sabbath by doing housework herself.

"You're a Papist, you can work," she said.

I was getting all tangled up inside. The twine was writhing and twisting in every direction.

"I was sick," I said. "I was sick when we were camping."

She looked down at me. My Auntie Theo was a large woman with a round pale face, short white tufty hair and heavy black eyebrows. She always wore big glasses and bright pink lipstick, and usually had a cigarette between her fingers or her lips. She reminded me of a panda. Even the way she moved was awkward and round-shouldered, with little paddling footsteps.

"What do you mean sick?" she asked. "Is it because of your monthlies?"

15

"I have a piece of twine in my stomach."

In fact it didn't feel like twine anymore but sharp and piercing like twigs, and the pain was nothing compared to the agony I felt when Auntie Theo leaned down, twisted her fingers in my tousled hair and yanked me upright.

"Listen to me you little wretch, you get into the house and start cleaning this minute," she said, crouching down so that I could feel the death beams flashing from the lenses of her pink-rimmed spectacles.

Behind her Dusty snarled. I hoped he was going to snap at her ankles, but she turned and glowered at him and he got up and crept across to the laurel hedge and took refuge under its glossy leaves.

I approached the house as if I was going to my execution. Her face was changing from pale wishy-washy to bright pink which was a forewarning of a major tantrum. I was the only person young enough for her to vent her bad temper on. When she had one of her rages she could do anything – box me in the face, push me into the dark under the stairs, threaten me with a knife or an axe, make me kneel down in a corner like a dunce in a old-fashioned school, dangle me upside down over the banisters. Now that I'd grown taller than she was most of these punishments were becoming obsolete, but she always seemed to dream up new ones which were even worse. She wasn't going to let me get on with the house cleaning without first inflicting some form of torture.
I walked into the hall ahead of her, expecting a blow on the back of my head, or my knees, or some sharp prod. I contemplated running straight through the hall and out the back door, or making a dash for the stairs and my bedroom where I'd keep her out with a chair propped under the door handle. The main thing was to keep my back to her. If she caught hold of my stomach I'd have to go through the agony of her fingers grabbing the end of the twine and wrenching it out of me. I placed my hands over the place where it was and felt it move down and settle in a hard knot in my groin. As I moved quickly forward Auntie Theo grabbed the swimsuit. The fabric pulled tightly against my body and pain stitched itself up and down my front.

At that moment the doorbell rang. I ducked under Auntie Theo's arm and ran to answer it, not caring about being nearly naked. I'd have opened it in my birthday suit to escape from her.

Mr Page was on the doorstep. He wanted to know when Daddy would be down. "Up in Dublin is he?" he winked at me. His breath smelled like the cabinet in the front room with all the bottles in it.

"Who is it?" Auntie Theo was right behind me.

Mr Page took a pack of cards out of his pocket and balanced them in his hand. "Ah, it's her Ladyship. And what are we all doing indoors on such a glorious day?" he asked. He always spoke to Auntie Theo as if he was acting in a play.

"Someone has been a bit unruly," Auntie Theo said.

Mr Page sighed. He held the pack of cards towards me and said, "Here Fran, pick one." I'd seen him do the three-card trick hundreds of times but I still couldn't figure it out. Today I felt too sore to do as he asked.

"No thank you," I said.

He looked surprised. "Everything alright? Anything I can do to help? I'm just visiting in the neighbourhood and thought I'd pop in."

"Everything is perfectly alright, thank you," Auntie Theo said in her snippiest voice as I slowly crumpled at Mr Page's feet, like a puppet when her central string, holding the rest of her together, snaps.

I had the piece of twine removed first thing the following morning by a surgeon. Afterwards they told me that appendicitis starts with vomiting, nausea, sometimes a pain that moves around from one area to another before finally settling where the appendix is located. They also told me that it's a part of our bodies that was left over from some stage in our evolution. It is of no use whatsoever, and nobody knows what its original function was. I was lucky I'd been caught before it burst. If it burst it would have poisoned my whole system and I would most likely have died.

"Did you find anything else inside me that didn't belong?" I asked the nurse who was examining my stitches.

She looked up at me as if she'd been bitten, and put a warning finger against her lips. Then she whispered that the year before a cross lady who was always complaining got an even worse pain after having her appendix removed. They brought her back to the theatre, reopened her and found that they'd left a scissors inside her.

It's just a lump. A thing. Mine was hard and swollen. That's what they told me, but I knew it was a long piece of cord covered with slime and most of it was still curled up in the pit of my tummy.

A BALL OF STRING

Myrna and myself were touring in Connemara when Fran had her appendix removed. I knew nothing about it until it was over.

The Connemara trip was my suggestion. I was feeling a bit down in the mouth. A large government contract I'd been awarded was scrapped without warning. The shock of finding that something I'd considered nicely tied-up and simply waiting for the Minister's go-ahead vanished leaving me at a loose end. Myrna was jubilant at the thought of taking a break. It was her birthday. Was it true that I'd remembered?

Of course it was I lied, replacing the telephone in its cradle and hurrying downtown to a shop that specialised in sexy underwear.

I put the package, gift-wrapped in silver paper patterned with shiny red hearts and gold stars and tied with black velvet ribbon, in the glove compartment of the Mercedes and went to collect my ladylove.

She was out on the footpath, complete with suitcase, looking like peaches and cream. She had a string of coloured beads around her neck and a new fluffy jumper, a tight white skirt, and strappy high-heeled sandals. We were seldom together outside the hotel and looking at her in the open air I thought how young, energetic and hopeful she was. The sun brought out the gold

19

glints in her curly hair and her hazel eyes sparkled. I caught myself dreaming about a new life, a fresh beginning. Myrna and myself on a sunkissed beach. My children grown up and done for. Fran would fit in somewhere, we might even bring her with us.

"Hi pet!" Myrna reached over and gave me a moist kiss on the cheek before I'd switched on the engine. Then she gave me a quick grope which reminded me of the scarlet nonsense nestling in the glove compartment and filled me with gleeful anticipation. We owed ourselves some fun.

It was late when we arrived at the hotel. Too late for dinner, but we'd stopped and eaten in a roadside pub. Some of the registration numbers in the car park were from Limerick. I entered the hotel cautiously, wary of being hailed by some inquisitive neighbour wanting to stick his nose into my private life. But there was nobody to be seen except the staff. I disliked the idea of tongues wagging about us. It would take the lustre from the whole escapade with Myrna and make it seem sordid and smutty.

Myrna herself was perfectly happy, entranced by our room, pleased with the night sounds coming from the surrounding woodlands. That night we slept like babies in each other's arms. It was only when I was woken by the dawn chorus of birds with Myrna's head resting heavily on my shoulder that I remembered the gift packet out in the car.

The day was glorious and we decided to take a trip up to Achill Island. We breakfasted in our room and left the hotel unseen. Myrna had never been to Achill and was as excited as a child. The fine weather had brought men out onto the bog to cut turf. I glanced at them as I drove, and remembered my father in my early childhood, helping out a country cousin, straightening up with great caution and rubbing his aching back. It had been more than 40 years since I'd walked across the undulating ground to give him a hand and tell him I'd passed my first exams.

Beside me, Myrna fiddled with the knobs on the car radio.

A signpost told us that we were close to Knock and, impulsively, we turned the car in that direction. It was still early in the day.

It was the beginning of May, not yet high season for pilgrims. The town itself was as well laid out as an American shopping mall. The neat new main street was lined with souvenir shops crammed with blackthorn sticks, log pictures, leprechauns and other brightly coloured junk. China vases in powder blue and candy pink, ornamental plates in every colour known in Hong Kong, glittering statuettes of saints, the Pope in profile and full-face the photo frames entwined with tinsel, ornamental dishes and bowls, enough rosary beads to reach the moon if laid end to end.

Myrna was dressed in a white off-shoulder top and her bright curls were tied back with an orange ribbon. As we passed display after gaudy display she suddenly embarked on a shopping spree, dodging into one small shop after another and emerging clutching fresh novelties. An Infant of Prague, rosaries, a holy water bottle shaped like the Mother of God, a holy water font, a picture of the Sacred Heart, a gold crucifix, a model of St. Peter's in Rome that lit up from inside and had not one, but two Popes – John Paul XXIII and Pope Pius XII. And medals – on chains, on key rings, in little plastic pouches.

"Hey," I protested, "what's all this for?"

"Fun," she said. "I never have time to shop. I never have time to do anything." She held up a mug with the current Pope on one side and the Vatican on the other. "Want this?"

"No thanks."

I wanted her. I'd been wanting her ever since we got here. Looking at her with her armload of religious baubles I wanted her more than ever. I became dizzy with lust. I took some of her packages and set off frantically, leading her away from the shops and down past rows of shuttered booths, newly-painted, ready to open when the regular summer devotions began. I tugged Myrna into the space between two of them, piled her purchases at our feet and kissed and fondled her until I felt her desire awaken and match my own.

21

We became ravening beasts. We moaned and sucked and arched and dipped. Finally we emerged, laughing, holding our packages in front of our disorderly clothes just as a coach with God's Bus displayed on its front and elderly wrinkled faces pressed against its dusty windows pulled into the parking lot beside us.

We hurried away from their curious looks, round to the back of the basilica. More elderly people were there, sitting in the open air, gazing at the glassed-in statues that marked the spot where the apparition was seen. Myrna sat down but I was more interested in studying the new building. I'd applied for the contract when the edifice was planned but hadn't even been called for an interview.

The basilica was octagonal. I imagined the construction headaches. The altar was situated in the centre. Everything was very modern and very functional. There were glass doors that slid back to admit and segregate crowds. I walked down to the Sacred Heart chapel and on to the confession boxes where Monsignor Horan's name hung from the first one. There was no light shining in front of any of them to indicate that there was a priest in attendance. I suddenly felt overwhelmed by a sense of dissatisfaction with myself, and sorrow for my dead wife, and remorse for any sin I might have committed with Myrna or any other woman or, for that matter, by myself. I knelt down in an empty pew and prayed for the peaceful repose of my wife, the well being of my children, and forgiveness for my own transgressions.

When we returned to the hotel for the second night I felt rather subdued. It was Myrna's actual birth date, but instead of giving her the lingerie I ordered champagne after our meal. Dom Perignon. £75.00 a bottle. The manager carried it to us, crooked in his arm like a newborn babe, smiling benevolently and asking, "A special occasion?"

"My birthday," Myrna said.

"Ah," his gaze took in myself and Myrna, our probable ages, my wedding ring, Myrna's lack of one, and he bowed, lips twitching, before uncorking the bubbly.

"Enjoy yerselves while ye can," he said before setting it in its holder.

"What a prick," Myrna said loud enough for him to hear as he walked away. Suddenly the only effervescence left was in the champagne. Like when a cloud suddenly obliterates the sun on what promised to be a perfect afternoon.

The next thing that happened was the arrival in the hotel bar, where we were having post-prandial brandies, of one of Myrna's clients. A foxy-faced politician who'd once been a government minister. He came in, casting his eye around for easy prey, and spotted us at once.

"Be the hokey farmer," he loped across hand out to press our flesh. "Isn't it far from home ye are. Is it a celebration? Have ye big news or something?" We'd ordered a second bottle of champagne and brought it with us from the table.

"It's my birthday," Myrna said.

"Well, and may you have many more of them darlin'." His gaze swept the bar a second time and saw no other catch as good as us. "I'll sit down and join ye," he said.

From then on the evening turned into a debacle. I couldn't even get drunk. The alcohol tasted like piss and had no effect on me. A few of the ex-minister's cronies arrived and were introduced with much clapping of shoulders and squinty-eyed glances. As the evening wore on someone sang a rebel song and was cheered to the roof. I sat glooming in my corner, the skeleton at the birthday party his eye sockets smarting from cigarette smoke. I sulked and failed to applaud when Myrna sang in her sturdy clear voice, *"She moved through the fair,"* and *"My love is like a red, red rose . . ."*

I thought regretfully of the silly gift in the car. There was no point in giving it to her now. Someone tapped my shoulder. I had a telephone call. They'd found me via Myrna's hotel. It was Alice, to tell me that Fran had just had her appendix removed.

The hotel was dark and silent by the time Myrna came to bed. I'd gone upstairs ahead of her after briefly telling her about Fran's operation. "That's awful," she said, but I wasn't even sure she'd heard me. I feigned sleep as she climbed in beside me and when she whispered my name I gave a loud snore that sounded as fake as a pantomime dame's.

Next day I arrived at St John's Hospital, Limerick, minus Myrna but with a miniscule G-string still, elegantly and expensively wrapped, scrunched into a ball in the glove compartment, and a pile of worthless religious trash in the boot and nobody to give any of it to.

VANISHING AND APPEARING ELEPHANTS

I imagined that white elephants were huge and luminously pale sacred beasts but Auntie Theo told me I was wrong.

"This is a white elephant, Fran," she said, picking up a lumpy cushion with a pink daisy chain stitched onto a yellow background. "And this," she held out a lopsided parchment lampshade with a blue fringe then dropped it into the big box that was being sent to her church's summer bazaar.

These treasures had been made by Lynda and Alice as presents for our mother years ago and now they were discarded. I didn't think that they should be given away. However, I said nothing. A lot of other things I considered special were also transformed into white elephants. A brown pottery jug with a woman's head on the stopper and Calvados in cream letters across the front. A dark-green pottery gazelle with paler green spots, a tambourine, a plaque made from Tunisian tiles glued onto white hardboard. These were souvenirs picked up by my parents on holidays before I was born. I liked to think of my mother choosing them. I liked to think that she and I would have admired the same things such as the dream catcher that Beth gave me for my birthday, or anything coloured dark blue and decorated with gold or one of my poems:

> *My dreams are lovely, dark and gold*
> *The catcher has them in its hold.*

25

Auntie Theo ran the white elephant stall for her church's summer bazaar. She was also very involved with the Bible-study group formed by members of the congregation. There were about twelve of them and they took turns meeting in each other's houses to pray, read passages from the Good Book, bear witness, and stuff their faces with sandwiches and cakes washed down by strong tea.

Billy Kelly, our housepainter, was there on the day that the big teapot turned into a white elephant.

"That crowd of crawthumpers," he said staring at the Bible-study group as they followed each other into our drawing room. He was painting the hall and stairs and they were holding a meeting in Riverview. This was something that happened quite often when Daddy was away. It was two weeks after my operation and I still felt sore sometimes. I wished that Billy Kelly wasn't present. Whenever he was around there were problems. That afternoon he began to sing Ave Maria, in a loud voice which made Auntie Theo poke an angry face out at him after she'd ushered in the group, and hiss, "Will you please BE QUIET!"

He came into the kitchen after me because he needed a mug of coffee before starting to work on the banisters. He was often at work in our house where something always needed a dab of paint.

"Any chance you could give me a tenner to go to a funeral?" he asked me, sitting down on the bench at the red table.

I shook my head, preoccupied with the details of preparing tea for the visitors. Auntie Theo was a stickler for correct hospitality. I had twelve teacups arranged on the wooden worktable and one mug for Billy's coffee on the formica one where he sat.

It was on afternoons like this that I made up stories about the sort of tea parties we'd have if my mother was alive. Balloons, iced cakes, gingerbread men, games of hide and seek, treasure hunts, conjurors, waltzing around the rooms and all the other things I'd read about in books.

"I don't have money," I said.

He snorted. "Can't you ask your aunt?"

"She'd kill me," I said, thinking of her and her friends talking to Jesus.

26

I was calculating how much tea was needed for 25 multiplied by two-and-a-half cups of tea and wondering if I should go and take the clothes in off the line in case it rained before the food had been served.

"I was at a funeral yesterday," Billy said as I gave him coffee and refilled the kettle to the brim for the tea. I continued about my tasks, trying to ignore him as he rattled on about the expense of drink and funerals. "The graveyard was full of nettles," he said. I had to look while he pulled up his trouser leg to show me the stings. The priests should be made cut them down. The one who said yesterday's Mass for the Dead was as brown as a Chinaman from holidays abroad.

When he stopped, the sound of hymn-singing wafted through from the drawing room. Billy made a rude noise. I stood on a chair to take down the huge brown teapot from the top shelf of the cupboard beside the refrigerator. It was one of the few items in our house that belonged to Auntie Theo. It had been passed down from her grandmother. It had survived the journey home from India and, old as it was, there wasn't a chip on it.

"Where did that yoke come from?" Billy asked.

"Auntie Theo's grandmother, my great-grandmother, brought it home from India," I said. I was proud of it. The grandmother was also Mummy's grandmother. My mother might have held this teapot, carefully, close to her chest just as I was doing at that moment.

"A Protestant teapot," he said. "What did she use it for?"

"Parties," I said taking out the lumps of sugar and emptying in half a pound of tea.

"Looks more like soup kitchens to me," he said. "That's all that crowd are ever up to. Paying people to join their church. Proselytizers, Protestants, they're one and the same."

I ignored him and got busy putting milk in the jugs and topping up the sugar bowls because as soon as the hymn-singing stopped the Bible-study group would want to eat. After they'd refreshed themselves they would start Bearing Witness, which often went on for hours. When they were finished a very holy woman called Sibyl, who was ancient and wore a shawl over her woollen coat even in summer, and large hats with veils, would read their fortunes in the tea leaves in their cups.

"It's an ignorant looking thing, that's what it is," Billy said as I gave the water in the brown pot a final stir before putting on the lid.

I stared at him. I was glad he was over at the other side of the kitchen. I hated the thought of him even breathing on the teapot which was part of my own mother's past.

I was only a few moments out of the kitchen. I had to carry in the cups and saucers and milk jugs and sugar bowls. The sandwiches and cakes were already laid out on the big marble coffee table. Tea knives and forks were folded in paper napkins, and a set placed on each china plate. The full group were present and they sat in silence as I moved around, trying not to stumble as I squeezed past bony ankles and big laps, and being careful not to knock off Sibyl's big black straw hat.

The company was mostly women. The two men were elderly. One had a wispy goat's beard, the other one a surgical boot which, once, to my huge embarrassment I'd fallen over.

Auntie Theo got up from the chair facing the door and began to pile stuff onto each person's plate as I set out the cups and saucers.

"Is the tea ready?" she clapped her hands when she'd finished. Her fingers were coloured orange from cigarettes. All of the Bible-study group smoked. It reminded me of the spirals of incense wafting upwards at a High Mass.

"I'll get it now," I said meekly and left the room.

Billy was back at his painting as I returned to the kitchen. He had released Dusty from the outhouse where he was kept locked up for these occasions because he hated the Bible people, especially the man with the surgical boot. The dog was lying at the foot of the stairs, his eyes fixed on the drawing-room door. Billy looked over his shoulder and winked as I started to take the animal back out again. As I came back in I heard him whistling *"Oh Queen of Heaven, the Ocean Star,"* and I hoped he'd soon stop. I'd dragged Dusty back into the outhouse on top of the potato sacks and pyramid of old paint tins and garden implements and left him there whining.

In the kitchen, as I approached the table, I stopped worrying about Dusty's whines, or Billy's whistling, because something much worse had happened. The lid of the teapot had disappeared. I'd put it on. I was sure I'd put it on before I went out. Of course, Billy had been interrupting me, but even so – I started pulling the place asunder, looking under the sink, on the windowsill, in drawers, in the cupboard where it was kept, in the refrigerator, in the grill pan, everywhere. Everywhere. I whirled like a dervish trying to find it.

"Francesca, hurry up!" Auntie Theo's voice boomed from the hallway.

I looked around in despair, then took a clean table napkin from a drawer, folded it into a square and placed it where the lid should be and went back to the Bible group.

It worked. I made my way carefully from person to person, crouching down and pouring very slowly so that the hot liquid did not slosh up through the napkin. I even fooled Auntie Theo, who was busily talking about God's grace to the man with the goatee beard and held out her cup without looking at me. I grew more relaxed. The awful ache in the pit of my tummy faded away. I'd have the teapot back on the shelf before the meeting was over. I'd be able to keep up the deception for months, years, even until my aunt was dead.

It was Sybil asking me about my operation that made the trick fall apart.

"We prayed for you in the meeting hall," she said. "Poor auntie was very worried."

I nodded, keeping my hand pressed on the napkin.

"Put down the teapot, dearie," Sybil beamed out from under her black brim. "You must look after yourself. Put it down there. It's heavy. You don't have to hold it all the time."

"It will mark the table," I said frantically.

"You can use this," a thick raffia mat materialised between my aunt's fag-stained fingers. Auntie Theo always listened in when people spoke to me.

"And we don't need this!" She leaned forward and removed the folded napkin with a flourish.

A gasp went up from the gathering. I even gasped with delayed shock myself.

"Francesca," Auntie Theo's voice dripped icicles. "What has happened to great-grandmother's teapot lid?"

What could I say? I stood willing the sheepskin rug under my feet to turn into a magic carpet and carry me away.

"You've broken it, haven't you? Wicked girl! You're as clumsy as a . . . as an . . ." Terrible words trembled in the air. I waited for her to say them, to say once again that I should be sent away to some place where I'd be taught how to behave, but a change came over her and she slowly got to her feet and began to tell of how, as a young girl, she had once thrown a book at her little sister Jane and it had broken a window and her little sister had been the one who got the beating because she hadn't owned up.

I knew by the rapt expressions of the group, Auntie Theo's clasped hands, and the way her voice came out in quick breathy rushes that made the pearls rise and fall on her bosom, this was private and I shouldn't be there. Sybil's hat kept nodding in assent. Mr Goat sat with his eyes closed behind his thick glasses, pulling at his beard. The man with the surgical boot stared sadly at the carpet. The other women sat with their shoulders hunched, peeping up at Auntie Theo from time to time. One of them wiped away a tear.

Back in the kitchen I resumed my search. I eventually found the vanished lid, or a few chips of it, in the waste bin. They were small, none of them bigger than my little finger nail, but the brown glaze had the familiar dull glow of antiquity. It had been broken by something hard, a rock, maybe, or a hammer. I found specks and white dust on the floor by the radiator.

It was a very long meeting. A lot of people must have borne

witness. It was after 7.00 and Billy was gone, still whistling his tune, when Auntie Theo called me in to clear everything away. The teapot lay with its yawning top in the middle of the scraps.

Sybil was the only person still with her. She smiled at me as I came in.

"I was just remarking to your aunt," she said, "that it's such a lovely shape it would be a pity not continue using it. Not for tea of course, but it would make a container for certain flower arrangements. Chrysanthemums and gladioli, or large bunches of white and purple lilac."

I watched as the teapot changed into a sacred monster. A big thing of little use, it's spout turned up as if it was going to start trumpeting Onward Christian Soldiers.

VANISHING AND APPEARING ELEPHANTS

What do you do if the woman you adore doesn't want to bear your child? You would do anything, anything in the world to spare her the least moment of distress. Then she tells you that in spite of taking every possible precaution – except the birth-control pill which brought on such unpleasant side effects as noises in her head, kidney infections, a rash, she had to stop taking it – she has been caught and is frantic.

We were walking in the woods in Garrykennedy when Jane told me that she wanted to get rid of the baby. We'd left Alice, Lynda and Josh back at the harbour, playing a game of soccer on the green with the children from the refurbished stone cottage beside the pub. Their mother was sitting on a campstool at the gate, hooking a rug.

"They'll be grand," she said, waving us off with her sewing needle. "They're big enough to look after themselves."

"That's just it, Henry," Jane said, walking ahead of me along the twisting path. "With a baby you have all those nappies, the pram – getting it up and down the front steps, me."

She stopped and looked up at the trees, "I can't bear it. Me turning into a bloody elephant all over again."

33

Before she made the announcement I'd been planning a holiday – just the two of us. Turkey seemed to be the place to go at the moment, or maybe Egypt – Cairo, Luxor, the Aswan Dam. Last year the children had been old enough to be left in the care of a responsible adult – Jane's sister, Theo, and we'd gone to Sicily, sat in the mellow Autumn evenings in the plaza in Taormina, made love in a *pensione* crammed with woodcarvings and a clock with a golden pendulum.

"I feel horrible about it," Jane said.

I felt anguish on her behalf. She was exaggerating of course, she was never enormous with child, just big.

"I've thought about it from every angle," Jane said. "Even if you don't agree I'm going to go to England and have an abortion. But, you'll have to give me the money, otherwise I'll hate you for the rest of my life."

"Are you really serious about this?" I asked, although her tense face and quivering lips were proof enough of her resolve.

She gave me a dark glance.

"It's not such a big thing, Henry. Not yet. But I'll need to go very soon, while it's safe."

I considered getting down on my knees on the muddy path and begging her to change her mind. And then I realised I was being hypocritical. My poor Jane! Why should she have to suffer just because of a cruel twist of fate? We weren't saints, we were a couple trying to bring up their children, we needed a better house before we added to our family. We needed a break. It was my fault if she was pregnant.

"I'll just crack up if I have to go through with it. You don't know how awful it is for a woman," Jane said, dragging her fingers through her sleek black hair. "I feel disgusting. I can't face it. All this business of getting bigger and clumsier. And for what? A little brat you can never escape from, ever."

I'd never heard her sound so bitter about anything.

I felt as bad as she did at the news. Worse in a way, because I was the beast, I was the one who had forced this thing on her. It would be selfish of me to compel her to do something she was totally set against.

34

"I should never have been a mother," she said.

"Come on," I said, "We have three great kids. You love them, I love them, I love you."

"That's not the point," she said.

I reached for her and she wheeled towards me as I propped myself against a tree trunk. She pressed her face against my shirt and moaned.

The pregnancy was a bolt in the blue. Once again I thought of how I'd been planning to surprise her with a really exotic holiday. We'd worked our backs off. It was time we spoiled ourselves a little. I didn't want another baby either. I tried to think of when it might have happened.

"It was the damn diaphragm. It didn't work," she said as if reading my mind and we both laughed a little.

I tried to think of something comforting to say, but it was Jane who did the talking.

Josh was starting school in September. At last she was going to have an hour or two each day she could call her own. Did I know how much that meant to her? Did I know how desperately she wanted to start writing again? Besides, she went on, "I do feel ill. I'm all nervy. I'm going to loathe this baby. It's only a sort of tadpole now and already I feel as if I've swallowed a tapeworm. I'm afraid of what I'll do if I don't get it taken care of."

Looking at her set and intractable expression I became terrified. There was no point in arguing with her. Something would have to be done.

It was Nat Page who gave me the contact number. I felt awkward about asking him because his marriage to Winnie was childless. However, he took it in his stride. Of course he knew of a good, reliable place – who didn't! He'd helped a young woman to go there within the past twelve months, "Wouldn't have done at all, Henry. If you know what I mean."

"How is she now?" I asked.

He looked at me squarely and said, "She's the grandest. Not a bother on her. Not that I have any truck with her these days. She's water under the bridge."

As for Jane: We were taking the right step. He was all for it. The poor girl had enough on her plate as it was. Who did I think I was – old Joe Kennedy, maybe? Well I'd need to get her set up in a better house before getting notions like that.

"I know that," I agreed. The house we lived in had been a Protestant girls' orphanage before we bought it. I'd soon given up plans for renovating the place. The costs were too high and the rooms awkwardly shaped. I planned to sell it on at a profit and find a house that really suited our needs.

Two weeks later Jane and I were together in the snappy bustle of London and the world seemed a brighter, sharper place. Jane was cheerful and determined. On the flight over she said that she didn't care if the childminder we'd found sat the children in front of the television all day. Holding hands, we toasted each other with gin and tonics.

I sat in a pub while Jane went for the termination. It was so early in the pregnancy that she didn't have to stay in the clinic overnight. After the required number of hours I abandoned my ham sandwich and half-empty pint of beer and took a taxi to the address. From there we went to the Cumberland Hotel. Due to an oversight we were booked into a double bed instead of twins. The room was overheated and the bed creaked at every movement. When I touched Jane after she'd lain down, she shivered violently and asked me to go away. I ordered her a light snack of coffee and toast from reception and after it had arrived I left her and prowled the wastes of the hotel. It was only 10.30 but the bars were all closed. I finished up sitting in the reception area sipping at melting ice cubes in a Styrofoam container.

Late in the night I crept in beside my wife. She smelt sour and moaned when I kissed her shoulder, but when I carefully put an arm around her she rested against me, her body curled in a foetal position that made me remember our children curled in their cribs, and brought images of half-formed creatures floating across my exhausted gaze like approaching nightmares. However by morning the worst was over. Jane moved gingerly around the room while we waited for our breakfast and said she was fine.

It was summertime. We'd arranged to stay on in England for a few days. The pretext of our trip was to visit a bachelor uncle of mine who was poorly. In fact, there was no such plan. I hadn't been in contact with him since my schooldays. He was probably dead.

On that first morning we took a tentative walk along Charing Cross Road, stopping now and then to peer at book displays. When I asked Jane how she felt her replies were neutral and composed. Everyone in the clinic had been kind. Apart from some bleeding she should have no after-effects. They'd given her pills to deal with any adverse reaction. She felt OK.

"Good." I tucked her hand under my arm. "A few days of the high life is what we need now."

Jane rested her head on my shoulder while pigeons cooed in Trafalgar Square.

"I'm glad it's over," she said.

So was I.

At lunchtime I collected a hired red Ford and we drove down to Windsor. I did a tour of the castle while Jane rested. Then I strolled through the town and over the little bridge into Eton.

Our hotel was a picturesque establishment so old that it had been designed by Christopher Wren. We took dinner there in a dining room with leafy green carpets and paler green walls. The Italian waiters hovered like guardian angels. Out on the patio a group of merrymakers drank beer with gusto. Jane looked very young and a little pale. She'd been 22 when we married ten years ago. Ten years and three children. Now Alice was nine, Lynda seven and Josh four-and-a-bit. I could understand her dismay at the thought of another child. Later, when we were more organised, we could try again.

I resolved to make an effort to get us out of our present home with its large draughty rooms. I had always been too busy with work to take time to do anything. We hadn't even installed central heating. In winter ice formed on the inside of our bedroom window. Mice scuttled permanently through the wastes of the unused basement.

The next house we owned would be a big place in its own grounds. There we'd have six more babies provided she wanted them. I was making good money. We could easily afford the right place if it turned up. It was what Jane deserved. And good central heating, and a hall door that wasn't reached by an awkward flight of steps. It was a miracle neither she nor the children had ever taken a serious fall.

I looked across the table at my lovely wife. She was poking her fork through the creamy sauce in which her veal had been cooked. Behind her a waiter hovered in suave attention. This last pregnancy had been a total miscalculation. Once again I reassured myself. She couldn't have been expected to go through with it. Josh's birth had made us a proper family. We had our two daughters and our son. There was no big rush.

Wine prickled in my gullet, mingling enticingly with the delicious food. Tomorrow we'd have fun looking at the waxworks. The weather forecast was terrific. We could head for Oxford. I wanted to see the old quadrangles and the newest additions and laugh at the hideous redbrick Victorian section. I'd bring Jane to see Holman Hunt's 'The Light of the World', hanging in deepest gloom in the chapel. She'd appreciate the joke. We were going to have a marvellous time.

I watched her pushing pieces of meat around. Her expression was pensive, her wine in her glass untouched. I leaned across the oak table and said, "We have all the rest of our lives ahead of us. As soon as we've got a large comfortable place to live in and you're good and ready we can try again."

Her weeping came on with the sudden force of a flash flood.

The waiters melted discreetly away and other diners pretended not to notice. When she'd stemmed the flow she whispered, "You haven't a clue, have you? It felt huge, Henry. I thought it'd only be a little thing, a speck, nothing at all. But it felt huge. And now there's nothing inside me but this monstrous space. I feel emptied out. I feel whatever I got rid of wants to trample me to death. I think I'll always, always, feel like this for the rest of my life."

THE GUILLOTINE

After the execution the three children, Alice, Lynda and Josh dipped their handkerchiefs in their mother's blood. They were immediately arrested and charged with making the situation worse. My father mourned in the sidelines. I was fast asleep in my cradle, missing all this. These were the kind of scenarios I was always making up. Everything was very serious and ceremonial.

None of my family ever discussed Mummy with me. All I got were hints. Beth Page knew no more than me about her death as we were the same age. The difference was that she'd been born years after her parents got married. Beth's mother told her that she'd been the best surprise of her whole life. Maybe that's what made me invent stories. I was jealous of the way Beth's mother thought she was so special. I just had Auntie Theo grumbling and giving out. Some children have imaginary friends. I had, I still have, an imaginary mother.

Science has proved that a head sliced off by a swift flash of a blade knows that it has been severed from its body whilst it rolls along the ground or into a basket. Consciousness survives long enough for such a perception, but hardly long enough for regrets. Did our mother perceive the three children with their clean hankies? Did she see me sleeping in my bassinette? I can't see that 'me' either.

Auntie Theo told me that Mummy went to heaven because she was too sad to live on earth. "It was your fault. She didn't want to have you," she said.

"That's not true!" I shouted helplessly, not wanting to believe her. "Prove it. How do You know?"

"Little children shouldn't ask questions about things they don't understand." She plodded over to the kitchen sink and poured herself out a glass of water while I tried to work up the courage to kick the backs of her fat legs.

You could build a Berlin Wall from all the 'shouldn't ask' questions in my life.

I figure that it takes even longer to kick a stool from under your feet than it does for a guillotine blade to fall. The actual beheading takes two hundred parts of a second. The time it takes for the blade to fall is one seventieth of a second. The power of a properly constructed guillotine blade when it stops at the bottom of the platform is 888.5lbs. Death by hanging is slower.

The last sense we lose is our hearing. She'd have heard the sparrows cheeping. They were always there, scavenging in the gutters at the back of the house. Their incessant din made it impossible for a woman whose nerves were still jangling after the birth of her daughter to rest. Sometimes she charged out into the yard and threw stones at them. It only made them noisier. Like the baby, who cried harder if she was lifted too impatiently from her cot. But somehow, I didn't like that story so I changed it. I was the favourite, after all. Daddy told me that they bought Riverview for me. They moved into it when I was three months old.

"And what happened to Mummy then?" I asked.

He sighed. "I don't know, Fran. I don't know. But you were special, honey. Don't let anyone ever tell you otherwise."

I loved the idea of moving to Riverview shortly after my birth because I was so special. But when I tried to picture my mother things grew muddled.

I imagine she heard the familiar creak of the back gate as the man arrived to deliver central heating oil, his footsteps on the earthen path, the dog before Dusty snarling across the yard. It was too late for her. The distant thud was the stool landing on its side. Her feet dangled in space as the man yelled for her to call off the animal.

It was Beth who told me that Mummy hanged herself. She'd heard her own mother telling Mr Page that the saddest day of her life was the day Jane Cleeve put the noose around her neck. "Did you know about that, Fran? Isn't it awful." Beth's face wobbled with sympathy.

At first I refused to believe her. Then I asked Auntie Theo straight out and she slapped me right across the face so I guessed it had to be true.

"I've always said you were nothing but trouble. They should have given you away," she said. But her eyes were darting behind her glasses like tiny fish in a bowl.

It was all very hush hush. "We don't talk about that," my sister Alice said when I asked her for details. "You're lucky you can't remember what it was like."

By the time I was almost thirteen, the year I had my appendix out, I'd stopped even trying to get an answer. I used to look at the Madonna picture on the landing and I felt that she, my mother, understood. We shared special secrets. Meanwhile my father was almost always away and Auntie Theo ran the house as if she was trying to win a world war. I spent most of my time with Beth and the older ones more or less did what they liked. If Auntie Theo wanted a target she used me.

Lynda celebrated her twenty-first birthday while Auntie Theo was away with her Bible-study group for a weekend in Kilkee. Every year they went away and stayed in a large house in the West End, facing the sea. We were put on good behaviour before she left. Naturally, it was a perfect time for a party.

This one started off excellently. We tied balloons to the banisters. Josh – who worked as a disc jockey – set up the music. There was shrimp dip, cocktail sausages, sandwiches, spicy chicken wings, a punch bowl and, of course, a birthday cake.

Beth came to keep me company. I wore red Dick Whittington boots that Daddy had given me the money for on my own birthday. Beth had a black velvet dress with a white organdy collar.

One thing about Lynda, she always knew lots of boys and all of them, except one, came to her party. Daddy was spending the weekend in his friend's hotel. "He wouldn't mind anyway," Lynda said. "But you two monkeys better not try anything bad like smoking or sneaking a glass of beer."

There was no danger of that. Beth and I thought drink was gross and the only time we smoked was when we pinched some of Mrs Page's and brought them up to the loft.

The two of us spent most of the first part of the evening in my bedroom, doing experiments with our hair, and practicing song-and-dance routines in front of the mirror. Then we played that game where you hide a hand behind your back, adopt one of three finger positions, and show your opponent. Scissors cuts paper, stone blunts scissors and paper wraps stone. I had a toothache I didn't want to tell Auntie Theo about and Beth tried a cure that her mother had shown her. She pressed hard against the root of the nail of the index finger on my right hand, but she mustn't have done it properly because my tooth kept on hurting. Next she examined my operation scar which was only a thin pink line. Eventually, there was nothing left to do but go down and face the party.

Things were going quite nicely. It was after 10.00 and the rooms were almost in darkness. Couples were moving around, some of them dancing, some of them huddled in groups, some of them just sitting with plates of food on their laps being serious and well-behaved. Josh was the only one who took any notice of Beth and myself. He asked us what record we'd like him to play and I let Beth choose. She asked him for a Boy George record called, 'Do you really want to hurt me?' When he put it on Alice started yelling at him to stop playing such crappy songs. He took no notice. The music was set up in the front room which was also the room where the piano was. Alice decided that she'd play the piano to drown out the sound of Boy George. She marched over, lifted the lid and didn't notice the cactus plant on the piano stool until she sat down on it.

After that things got a bit wild. Alice, who was usually timid, started jumping around the place screaming, "Oh my bum, my bum." The plant was still embedded in her and it must have been really sore. Someone said cactus plants were poisonous. One of the boys said, "If she lets me take off her panties I'll make her better. OK Alice?"

I was getting a pain in my tummy as if the ball of twine was back. It was because I'd tasted the punch in the punch bowl. It tasted truly disgusting. Lynda brought a dazed Alice off to have her cactus wound attended to. Josh put on some really loud music and everyone began to jump around. I noticed that the cupboard where Daddy kept the liquor was open and some of the bottles had been taken out.

My sisters came back and Josh put on quieter music, and some of the boys brought in cans of beer and cider from the boots of their cars. Alice had a boyfriend called Mark who was like herself, quiet and conservative. He hadn't taken any part in the rumpus about the cactus plant. When Alice came back after dealing with the poisonous needles I saw them sitting down with their arms around each other, beer cans in their hands. Lynda was the rackety one. As the party got under way she was the centre of a rowdy group who started fooling around grabbing each other and sometimes getting into a clinch and sneaking out to the kitchen. Josh was always the loner, like a displaced person. He just kept on fixing the music, taking an occasional swig of beer, and puffing on one of his sweet-smelling cigarettes. Beth and I kept busy checking the candles, snuffing out the ones that were nearly finished and replacing them with new ones. We kept one eye on the couples slipping out to the back room which was where we did our homework and not much else. On the night of the party there were extra chairs in there, and a rug on the old sofa and cushions on the floor. As I slipped across the hall to get some lemonade in the kitchen I tuned into the gurgles and moans coming from behind the closed door. A girl's voice squealed, "No! I don't want to." A boy said something in an urgent voice. I had a vision of Auntie Theo appearing and walking in on top of them.

Later I noticed Lynda on the bottom steps of the stairs with a big guy in a red sweater sort of kneeling on top of her. I was the only person who'd heard the bell and was on my way to answer the door. As I put my hand on the latch to pull it open I suddenly thought it must be Auntie Theo and almost died of fright. However, it was the kissogram boy.

We'd all forgotten about the kissogram. It had been Alice's idea. A friend of Mark's wanted to be an actor and was trying to get some money together for drama school. He was making quite a lot by turning up at celebrations in fancy dress and serenading the guest of honour. Even though I was in on the plan to have him along for Lynda I couldn't think, for a moment, who the lean dark boy, like a French filmstar, was. He marched into the front hall and flicked his eyes around.

"Where is she?" he asked.

He had amazing black eyelashes. I was struck by his beauty immediately. It made me conscious of my new Dick Whittington boots and I forgot all about my toothache. However, he took no notice of me and walked past me with long steady strides, straight to where Lynda was being soppy with the boy on the stairs. He caught the boy by the back of his red jumper and yanked him up. The boy's fat sweaty face wore a look of surprise, and when he yelled in protest spittle shot out of his mouth. He was pudgy with fat hands and I wondered how Lynda could bear to have him touch her.

"Have I interrupted something?" Kissogram said, looking down at Lynda.

She leaned back, her party dress rucked up over her knees, her mouth half-open, and an expression of total surprise on her face.

"Oh my god!" she said.

They stared into each other's eyes and the kissogram boy said, "You fucking bitch."

Everything had gone very quiet, like when an angel is passing. Even Josh had turned off the music. The guests crowded in the doorways of the rooms, watching.

The new arrival and Lynda kept on staring at each other. Then the boy seemed to remember where he was and why. He held out his hand and Lynda reached for it. Very slowly he led her into the front room, while as many people as could fit crammed in behind them. Beth and I were right in front. I could see the wide grin on Lynda's face.

"Some space please," the gorgeous boy said and we obediently backed away, leaving room in the middle of the carpet.

Lynda had disentangled herself from his grasp and perched herself on the arm of a chair and was staring at him as if she thought he was a snake. He opened his dark trench coat and threw it off in one quick movement. Underneath he was wearing a tiny leopard skin which just about covered his bulge, and showed off his muscles and his tan, and his ribcage. He was lean with a long smooth back and a small shadow of black hairs on his chest. I could feel my heart racing with admiration.

"Me Tarzan, you Jane," he said to Lynda who gave a silly scream of laughter.

Then he picked her up threw her over his shoulder, swung her down between his legs as if she was as light as a feather, left her lying on the ground and flexed his muscles. The next thing he did took us all by surprise. He jumped around holding out his arms asking people to feel how strong they were and clenching his fist as if he was going to punch someone in the face. He went over to the boy in the red jumper who backed away and nearly fell into the fireplace so that everyone laughed. Then he turned back to Lynda, picked her up again and, charging through the group made straight for the stairs. Everyone was in stitches by this time. He turned the corner for the second flight of stairs and everyone, except Lynda, was still laughing. Then we heard a bedroom door slam.

After that the party sort of ran down. Some of the people went home. Josh found a bottle of Drambuie in the drinks cupboard and mixed it with a can of Guinness and showed us a trick with tiny liquor glasses. You poured the mixture into them, set it alight then pressed the rim of the glass against the palm of your hand. It stuck tight and only burned your skin a little. After a second you pulled it off, it was like peeling off sellotape, and drank the mixture in one gulp. Beth and I only tried it once, but the rest of them were still at it as we crept out of the room.

Next morning I was woken by Lynda shaking my shoulder. I opened my eyes and found her standing beside my bed, a scissors in her hand. She put her finger to her lips and keeping her eyes fixed on mine sawed off a thick lock of hair which she put into a paper bag and slipped under my pillow. Beth, in the other bed, never stirred.

Her cheeks were very flushed with excitement and her eyes gleamed. I looked at her, feeling terrified.

"You mean, she left without as much as an explanation," Auntie Theo said when she got back from Kilkee.

I nodded.

"Disappeared into the blue. Where has she gone – China . . . Timbuctoo? What else went on in my absence?"

"Nothing," I said. "Nothing."

All of us had spent the day erasing the signs of the party, but when Auntie Theo arrived I was the only person in the place.

"Did you go to Mass, Francesca?" she asked after I'd told her about Lynda. I always had to give her a full report on my religious life. She even tried to make me tell her what sins I'd told in confession.

"Of course I went to Mass," I said.

She claimed that I showed signs of becoming a depraved person.

"What was the gospel?"

"The Road to Emmaus. They recognised him in the breaking of the bread," I gabbled. I'd taken the precaution of slipping down to the church in the afternoon and checking the mass leaflet for the day.

Some time later, when the whole Lynda story came out, it was taken as further proof of my sinfulness. I must have known about this upstart she'd run away with. I should have spoken up while there was time to save her. It was clear that I'd been a willing accomplice. The hair in the envelope she'd slipped under my pillow was proof of my wickedness. When I said I didn't know why she'd left me the keepsake and was totally surprised by the whole business I was accused of being a hypocrite as well as a liar.

GUILLOTINE

"Put a paper bag over their heads and they're all the same," was one of Nat Page's dictums about women. He had a lot of similar hard-chaw theories. The sort of stuff that men went along with at that particular time, especially if they were totally turned off by attitudes women were adopting – such as finding harmless compliments sexist, or flaunting hairy legs, or demanding that men share all the housekeeping. "If that's what they want they've got the wrong man here," he'd say. He also believed that sex on the side was a natural and deserved part of a man's life, whereas women, by which he meant wives, were much better off if they didn't play around. "If Winnie two-timed me I'd be gone," he'd say. "Not that she ever would."

I took his advice about women in the period after Jane's death. I didn't much care what the lady looked like, she wasn't Jane and so she didn't count. But I was hungry for nipples of all shapes and colours, the female form in every mould and dimension, but preferably comfy as goose down. I needed that curve of hip and waist, the mounds and hollows, the flowering of female flesh. I offered false sacrifices to their cunts and arseholes. I fell on each new woman the way a hungry infant latches onto his mother's breast. I clutched at them, keeping myself afloat. Then I met Myrna.

She was the first woman, after Jane, that was a person as well as a sex object. When, after the unsatisfactory trip to Connemara, I thought I'd lost her it made her even more precious. I spent serious time and effort wooing my way back into her good graces. I told her I'd do anything she wanted. I said she could make her choice, break it off or make up. Whichever it was I only asked one thing, that it be painless and quick.

I'd read about a husband who built his wife a guillotine for their haunt. If Myrna wanted to guillotine me I'd build one for her and all she'd have to do was pull the rope and I'd be gone out of her life forever.

We were in the hotel kitchen and Myrna was cutting a piece of sandpaper with a large scissors. She put it down, sashayed across the tile floor, wound her warm plump arms around my neck and kissed me. "It wasn't your fault Fran got appendicitis," she said.

Her lips tasted like sweet plums. I stroked her hair back from her forehead and kissed her again. Instead of going down to Limerick I stayed on in Dublin for the weekend and things were good between us.

I remained on to do some work during the week. It was Tuesday when Alice telephoned me at the office to ask if I'd heard from Lynda. She'd been missing since Sunday morning. I was taken aback. There seemed to be a boy involved. "Well damn," I said, "What's your Auntie Theo doing about it?"

"She was away," Alice said.

I sighed, feeling at a loss. When I got back to Myrna's place I worried out loud about my daughter's disappearance.

"What age is she?" Myrna asked.

I thought for a minute. I wasn't too sure. "Nineteen or twenty," I said.

Myrna laughed. "She's old enough to look after herself," she said cheerfully.

I supposed that she was. Even so, I felt uneasy. I found it hard to equate the small blonde girl with bright hazel eyes, who seemed to bounce instead of walk, with someone who had suddenly, behind my back, become old enough to be self-sufficient.

Nat Page had a fund of jokes. Some of them I'd heard twenty times too often. One was a guillotine joke. The priest rests his head on the block and when the rope is pulled the blade doesn't fall and he thanks Divine Providence for saving him. The lawyer has the same experience and is spared when he claims that it is unlawful to be executed twice for the same crime. The sucker engineer looks up at the release mechanism before putting his head in place and says, "Wait a minute. I see your problem."

I thought I'd helped Jane solve her problems. When we got back from London I took her air of despondency to be a natural after-effect which would disappear in time. And, quite soon it did. Business was thriving, and it involved a good deal of social activity – dinners, dances, cocktail parties, openings, charity auctions, buffet suppers, you name it. There never seemed to be much time to house hunt.

Most of the time we went to these events in a foursome with Nat and Winnie Page. Jane needed a large gin and tonic before facing out of the house, but that was understandable after a day cooking dinner and collecting kids. At least she wasn't pregnant. And money was rolling in. The perfect house had not yet turned up, but it would. Every week new residences appeared on the market. We were going through one of those times when a group of key figures all quit the scene within a short period and a whole new order is installed before anyone has noticed.

Nat Page assisted me in my search. He, himself, was comfortably installed in a fine red- brick Edwardian villa on the Ennis Road. The only snag was the mother-in-law who naturally stayed in residence when he and Winnie moved in after old Mr Quill died.

In spite of having enough money, my dream house didn't turn

up as quickly as I'd hoped. Something always went wrong at the last minute. Another buyer stepped in and bid the property up to an outlandish price. I was too well up in the construction business to be happy about buying an overpriced house just because it had some trendy addition like a sauna or Italian marble fireplaces, or a kitchen floor newly tiled in warm Mediterranean colours, or a split-level living room. I wanted a home, preferably old, full of character and craftsmanship.

In the meantime something bad happened to Jane. It began with whimpering in her sleep. Then it developed into moaning and weeping on a nightly basis. Even a large whiskey before going to bed didn't help. She tried sleeping pills, but they made her worse.

"What is it?" I asked cradling her in my arms and wondering how I'd face the two heavy meetings I had in the morning.

She shook her head, her face terror stricken. "It's nothing. It's me!"

Finally, after several weeks of this, in which I woke up most days feeling I'd been hanged, drawn and quartered, she opened her heart.

It was London. We shouldn't have gone there. She knew the minute the clinic door closed behind her that she'd walked into a trap. Even so she allowed them to cajole her into the theatre. She voluntarily removed her clothes and climbed onto the low operating table. Then they stepped forward and locked her down at the waist by stocks so that she couldn't move. With her eyes wide open she saw a bow saw descend from the ceiling and cut completely through her body. It didn't hurt, but she heard the crunch of bone, smelt fresh blood.

After some time she was requested to raise her head. She did so and found a completely examinable saw encircling her waist. Its blade was so sharp that the skin of her fingers flinched when she tried to touch it.

"I'm not there any more," she said, taking my hand and guiding it down between her legs where everything felt moist and warm.

I tried to tell her that it was an illusion. She'd had a bad dream. She was whole and complete, a desirable and pliant woman, but she refused to be convinced. I gripped her arms and her upper body became rigid and tense, but her lower body continued to welcome me. After a short bout of mild, amateurish wrestling I entered her. She moaned. Her orgasm matched my own heart-shaking explosion of terror and delight. Afterwards we lay together drenched with sweat and semen, our legs entwined. But her face, as I stroked her cheek and looked at her in the rosy glow of the bedside lamp, was stern and impassive.

After this the bad dreams became more infrequent and finally disappeared. Our sex life became, once again, normal and fulfilling. Weeks became months, became years. Then, amazingly, Winnie Page became pregnant after years of childlessness. At the same time Jane discovered that she too was pregnant.

"I really want this, Henry. I'm not upset at all. There's Winnie to keep me company," she said as if she thought I might object. "I think it's right for me to have another child. It makes up for last time and I feel that the house we want is going to turn up."

That was the closest we'd got to mentioning the trip to London in a quite a while. Jane's attitude to the new pregnancy made me feel that the whole unfortunate business was well and truly over.

I was on my way to the off-licence to order the Christmas booze when I saw the Virgin Mary. It was to be our last Christmas in the Edwardian terraced house. Francesca was three weeks old. Winnie also had a baby daughter. I was already making tentative plans to buy a Georgian mansion called Riverview, but had said nothing to Jane in case it fell through.

The statue glided over the traffic. It tilted slightly as it balanced on a funereal-looking wreath of green laurel leaves and yellow and white chrysanthemums. It was being carried along on the roof of a small blue Fiat car. Behind the car a lean wild-haired man carried a large crucified Christ. Beside him a young boy balanced a picture of the Sacred Heart that looked as if it had just been taken from someone's front hall. It had a sprig of holly stuck to its frame. There was no priest with them, but they were followed by a straggle of people, mostly women, carrying candles and shading the flames with the palms of their hands. Goose pimples rose on the back of my neck when I saw that the woman closest to where I stood was Jane. In her fox fur jacket, elegant green woollen suit and smart brown boots she stood out against the shabbiness of the other worshippers. I called out to her but she continued on without giving me a glance. Her lips moved, answering the responses to the rosary which was being led by somebody in a red van with a loudspeaker. The van was followed by two men carrying a banner that proclaimed, The Feast of the Immaculate Conception.

There was a mixture of comments, aspirations, complaints and mild jeering as they passed. The traffic ground to a halt and the horn-blowing grew louder and more impatient. I could see the statue wobble as it turned to head down Roche's Street where it was guaranteed to cause a major disruption. I thought of following them, of pulling Jane out of the group, asking her what she thought she was doing. But the sad severity I'd seen on her face reminded me vividly of the first time we'd made love after our London trip, the business of her nightmares, the saw that cut her in half and the bad patch in our lives.

"Did you see me in town today?" I asked her at suppertime. "No."

Her answer was swift and dismissive. I left it at that.

ROLLER-COASTER

Auntie Theo was my roller coaster. Big dipper is maybe a better title. From my earliest memories she loomed hugely in my life. Even by the time I was twelve, and able to look down on her she felt large. She couldn't be argued with. Confronted by her I became dumb. I lost my wits. Every so often she ploughed down a deep incline bringing me with her and I clung on expecting to be crushed to death at any moment.

For a short time, in the immediate aftermath of Lynda's flight from home, she left me alone. She was busy with the Bible-study group, collecting jumble for their bazaar. The school summer term had started. I had to study for the end of year exams. I was only forced to do heavy housework on Saturdays and in the evenings after my homework was finished. Then, under her supervision, I built my character by scrubbing out cupboards, weeding flower beds, polishing the brass door knocker, whose lion's head glared at me with the same ferocity as Auntie Theo did. And of course, before I left for school I had to take the clothes from the washing machine and hang them on the whirligig line, and as soon as I arrived home I had to check if they were dry and put them into the ironing basket.

Sometimes, as a treat, I was allowed to go to Beth's house to study. I'd walk there straight from school and we'd sit in Beth's bedroom with its bright rugs and crunchy lace curtains. After we'd worked for a while we'd amuse ourselves. We'd make beads from paper by cutting pages from old exercise books into strips. Then we'd spread glue on one side and roll them around one of Mrs Page's knitting needles. When they were dry we'd slip them off, paint them and string them into necklaces or bracelets. We were hoping to sell them in the Saturday market when we had enough made.

When we were bored with making beads we played love, like, hate, adore. This was a pencil and paper game in which you noted down emotions and matched them to colours then wrote a person's name under the pairings. The paper was folded so that only the emotion was visible, next the colour, finally the name. The trick was to get the other person to admit to unsuitable feelings towards someone. For instance, I would try to trick Beth into adoring Josh. Or she might succeed in getting me to hate the colour grey, and then she'd reveal the name of my favourite nun, Sister Dorothea.

Auntie Theo's indulgence towards me never lasted. Soon the bazaar was over. They'd made much less money for the heathens than on previous years. An early heat wave had sent people away to the seaside that Saturday. Auntie Theo had displayed the lidless brown teapot, with some branches of lilac from the garden to show its new function, at a sacrifice price. Nobody made an offer. She came home with it and watched while I got up on a chair to place it on the shelf in the high cupboard, its lustre as well as its top destroyed. I was wearing shorts because of the heat and she gave me a stinging blow across my calves before I climbed down.

I held the back of the chair and stepped gingerly onto the ground, then turned to face her. She was in a rage. Her head wobbled, and her mouth twitched. She fumbled in her cardigan pocket and produced the bag holding Lynda's lock of hair.

"What's this, you deceitful girl?"

She shook it at me.

"You knew, all about it, didn't you?"

I pressed my back against the refrigerator, shaking my head. I hadn't known what to do with the unasked for keepsake. I was afraid to throw it away because I had an uneasy feeling that if I did so I'd bring harm to Lynda. Instead, I put it in the small bamboo cupboard in my room where I kept keepsakes.

Auntie Theo moved close to me and I got the sweet fruity smell of port wine.

"Do you know that I've sacrificed my life for you?" she said. Boozy spittle landed on my cheek and I lifted my hand to wipe my face. She grabbed my wrist. "You little Papist. You little heathen. You're bent on becoming the scourge of your aunt."

I had grown taller than she was and I could have pushed her away but I was too frightened of her. She had no right to bully me. I should have complained to someone – Sister Dorothea . . . Mrs Page . . . Daddy years ago. But I hadn't. I'd let her pile all sorts of things onto me. I'd stood at the ironing board trying to iron the shirt blouses she wore under her navy costume for visiting until my knees were ready to buckle. I'd pleaded forgiveness when a button flew off. I'd admitted my wickedness when, in spite of my best efforts, the collars of the blouses turned up at the tips or developed irremovable creases on their cuffs or the back of the neck.

My sisters and brother could have helped, but none of them ever did. They were too busy with their own lives. It was easier to turn a blind eye, a deaf ear and leave me at her mercy.

After she'd shown me Lynda's hair I let her box my ears without retaliating, even though I immediately felt them grow puffy and tender and a sound like a knife scraping glass started in my head. Dusty, knowing I was in trouble, whined and scraped at the back door.

"She's gone to England, hasn't she," Auntie Theo kept chanting. "She's gone to England, hasn't she? She's gone to England."

"I don't know," I wept. "I swear I don't know. I don't know anything."

My eardrums were exploding.

"God will punish her," Auntie Theo said savagely.

I watched her gather herself to make another assault on me. I wished I'd been warned about the unsatisfactory bazaar. Then I could have hidden myself in the black hole. This secret place was a cellar Josh had shown me in one of his rare moments of realising I existed. It was reached by removing a false wall at the back of the cupboard under the stairs and climbing down a small ladder. I was always a bit frightened down there. I felt like Anne Frank, in Amsterdam. Any moment I'd be discovered and dispatched to my tragic fate. But it was better to be frightened than attacked by an Auntie Theo impersonating a battering ram.

As I braced myself for her next charge she stopped short, pressed her clenched fist against her chest and, with a surprised expression, gave a loud belch. A gust of smoky, winy gas flew into my face. My eyes felt itchy. I craved fresh air and cleanness.

After belching she seemed to deflate as if all the energy had been sapped out of her. It struck me that my indomitable aunt was growing old. I had no idea of her age, but she had been a good deal older than Mummy.

"I'll deal with you later," she said, giving me a nasty look. Then she hurried out of the kitchen, snorting as she went. Five minutes later I heard her snores through the closed drawing room door where she had sequestered herself for a snooze.

The paper bag with Lynda's hair had been left on the telephone table in the hall. I picked it up as gingerly as if it held a poisonous snake and tiptoed out to the cupboard under the stairs. There I released the catch, pulled back the false wall and climbed down. I tucked the bag of hair into a niche. Cobwebs brushed my face like corpse fingers. My heart began to thump. I got out again as fast as I could before the pookah woke up, or the ghost train came rattling through with all the skeletons shrieking at the faint-hearted girl who was so scared of a silly old battle axe.

"What colour, Fran?"

I came back to the loft and Beth.

"Pink."

"You don't hate pink."

I didn't but I was sure Beth had written Auntie Theo's name underneath it.

"Oh, gosh. You hate Lynda."

No I didn't. Lynda was the kindest of the three. When she left there was only Alice and Josh between myself and Auntie Theo. Alice was planning to marry Mark in two or three years' time. She was already buying magazines about Brides and Weddings. And Josh came and went at all hours, with his walkman and headphones so that even when he was there his mind was trapped on its own roller-coaster.

While Auntie Theo snored I went upstairs and changed into running shorts. Then I got Dusty's lead and we set out for a long fast walk: up Rose's Avenue, left past the Gaelic Sports grounds, up the long sloping wide road, then through the maze of modern houses with all their different gardens, ornaments, porches, curtains, a model ship on a window sill, a stone shoe full of geraniums beside a garden seat. I circled roundabouts, turned corners, marched along until sweat streamed into my eyes and down my sides and Dusty sat down, hoping I'd pick him up and carry him under my arm.

When I returned to Riverview tugging him behind me I'd cooled down and my clothes were clammy. I had just enough energy to unlatch Dusty's collar. I walked indoors on buckling legs and found Auntie Theo standing in the hall.

"I was overtired and so perhaps spoke hastily," she said, which, for her, was unusual.

I got the ball of twine pain in my tummy as I tried not to appear smug.

"You're bleeding," she said, her eyes widening in dismay. "All down your leg. Look, Francesca, blood."

I looked and saw the crimson trickle zigzagging from under the leg of my shorts. I felt surprised. There had been no briars, no sharp things, only houses and gardens. Then I remembered that it was a month since I'd had my period.

Auntie Theo became officious, marching upstairs and returning with a package which she held out to me. "Some pads," she said stiffly. "I suppose you know what to do."

I took the packages from her awkwardly. I hadn't mentioned the previous time, and the tampons, and Alice's instructions. I wasn't going to now. I went upstairs feeling dizzy and slow as if I was walking on the moon.

ROLLER-COASTER

The condition of the road from Doon Lake to Broadford was highlighted at a meeting of Clare County Council where it was compared to a roller-coaster ride. It was held in an Ennis hotel and I was present to offer my professional advice. There was a proposal that money allocated for the stretch of road in two years time be brought forward so that repairs could begin immediately.

Some arguing took place as to whether the road should be repaired or left as a foundation and a completely new road built over it. I explained to them that under the national roadwork programme that stretch had already been scheduled for reconstruction on the given date and so they had no discretion in the matter with regard to bringing the work forward. The road was not going to be touched in the foreseeable future. A small sum would be allocated for the most essential repairs, but the roller-coaster would continue to undulate over a mile or so on which motorists seemed determined to break the speed limit, despite its bad condition. One or two people at the meeting tried to protest. One of them insisted that it was not safe for general traffic. Another person said that it should be closed off until work was carried out. Someone else protested that if it was, diverted traffic would take an even more hazardous route along bog roads that were even more broken up and composed entirely of hairpin bends. The meeting ended when one of the councillors reminded everyone that attempts to patch up the bad part might result in the overall plan being sidelined.

Two days later, along the particular stretch that was the subject of the debate Nat Page put his foot down on the accelerator of his BMW. The car became airborne for a moment and then with a succession of booms, bangs and impossible twists, like a car in a funfair, plunged into the bog, tunnelling a furrow which pressed in on Nat's side of the bodywork, but leaving the young woman passenger enough space to push open the door on her side, scramble out and struggle across the rough surface to the road.

After a short while a tractor with a man bouncing on its seat appeared. The young woman, who was hysterical, flagged him down. They returned to the car and found that water had seeped into it up to the roof, drowning Nat who, probably, had been knocked unconscious by the impact.

I was in Limerick when the accident happened. Little bits of information filtered through the life of the city that afternoon. There'd been a crash in East Clare. Several people, or none, or one, were dead. Nat's name was mentioned. Somebody phoned my own place of business asking if I was in. When they were put through to me they said they'd called because they'd heard from a reliable source that I'd been killed along with Nat Page when the car we were travelling in hit a stone wall. Somebody else phoned the Page's house and got no reply. I telephoned Nat's office and was told that he'd gone out for the afternoon. By news time at 6.00 the facts had been verified. Nat's body was in the morgue of the Regional Hospital. His car was a write-off. The guards were appealing for witnesses, especially the young woman who had been travelling with him but she had done a vanishing trick.

I'd stayed on in Limerick after the meeting in Ennis. Suddenly it seemed as if fate had arranged everything and I was one of her pawns. I'd been complacent and worldly wise as I explained government policy to the Council. I'd reasoned with those who'd been the strongest advocates of some repairs. I'd talked them out of it. Now Nat was dead. The road had been declared highly dangerous and closed off to traffic. I had lost the one I rated my closest friend.

My worries about Lynda faded into insignificance. Three weeks had passed without news from her. Nobody seemed to know where she might be. Or, if they knew they weren't telling. Theo, clearly, was completely in the dark. A fact which ruffled her and caused her to utter dark comments about "unclean vessels" and "lost souls".

"I wash my hands of that girl," she said to me. "I can't take responsibility for the actions of a wilful young hussy. I always go on the trip with the Bible-study group. It is wrong to blame me for negligence."

"I'm not blaming you for anything, Theo," I said.

She glared at me while blowing smoke through her nostrils like a dragon before throwing the end of her cigarette into the fireplace.

I stepped into Jury's Hotel, automatically looking at the counter where Nat should be sitting on a barstool and was hit once again by the cruel fact of his death. I sat alone and ordered a cup of coffee. A man came along, lifted himself onto the seat beside mine and said, "Desperate, isn't it?"

I nodded, feeling sombre. I'd just come from the hospital where Nat's corpse was laid out under a cellular blanket in a room that brought shivers into my soul as I was transported back to the time when Jane lay waiting for me in the same place. The walls were the same shade of pale custard, the feelings of disbelief and the horror just as strong. The glass of the high-frosted windows cast the same chilling glow. And there was Nat with his best poker face, composed and secretive, like when he was about to pull off some big deal.

I needed a coffee to help me screw up the strength to call to the house and speak to Winnie. It was 8.00 in the evening and she'd be receiving the usual sympathisers – neighbours, casual associates, compulsive funeral goers. I remembered the stream of people when Jane died. The faces blurring into one face, the suffocating press of people who had known her, the whispers out in the hall.

"Did you know who the one with him was?" the man beside me intruded on my thoughts.

"Haven't a clue," I said.

"He was a hoor for the women."

He cocked his head to give me a sideways glance inviting confidences but I refused to be drawn.

"There's more to it than women, of course," he said.

I got down, leaving most of my coffee and headed out to Winnie.

She and her mother sat holding court while Beth threaded her way through the company like a sad little ghost holding out trays of sandwiches. The person sitting beside Winnie stood up to let me take my place beside her. I kissed her lips, sat down and took her hand. It was a block of ice. Mrs Quill was in the other section of the room. The folding doors were open and people threaded their way from one end to the other murmuring about the accident and similar tragedies and the general state of the country.

Winnie said to me: "You were like a brother to him, Henry. He thought the world of you."

Beth sidled up to us holding out a cup of coffee. The cup rattled in the saucer and the liquid splashed onto her dress. "Poor Daddy," she said and began to cry.

I took the cup from her and put it on a side table.

I started to get up, but Winnie tugged at my jacket for me to remain sitting down beside her.

"Help me, Henry. I can't bear it," she whispered.

"What do you mean?"

"Mummy says everyone believes that he had a woman with him. She says it wasn't the first time. He was always . . ." Her voice broke, ". . . two-timing me."

"What do you think?" I looked at her steadily.

Winnie knitted her strong eyebrows. I thought of Nat and his peccadilloes, the chances he took, the time he advised me about the London clinic for Jane, the good advice he'd given me about money. And there were other memories – business breakthroughs, drinking bouts, sprees, his solid support when Jane died.

"He's not coming back," Winnie said. There was a catch in her voice.

"Tell your mother she's talking through one of her fancy hats," I said.

"Yes," she said. "I suppose. She never liked him."

I looked over at Mrs Quill and her coven of friends. They were all gabbling nineteen to the dozen. I imagined Nat rising up from his deathbed and telling her to go to hell. Then the shock of his loss hit me again and made the bottom fall out of my stomach and sent me plunging into the depths. He was the sort of person you expected to last forever.

In Riverview a postcard had arrived with a picture of an amusement park, and a message: Hello from Blackpool. Will write when we have a permanent address. Love, Lynda.

"Who's we?" I asked.

There was a slight frisson around the kitchen table where the girls were sitting subdued and upset by Nat's death. Alice looked at me hard and said, "Just a friend."

I asked no more questions. I was too aware of my own deficiencies as a father.

"Did you see Beth?" Fran asked me. She looked tearstained.

"I did," I said. "And her mother."

"Is Beth alright?"

"She will be," I said.

Once again I was overcome by a feeling of utter disbelief. I'd spoken on the phone to Nat yesterday morning. We'd had an appointment to meet in Jury's bar at 6.00 this evening. He had papers for me to sign. I should be on my way to Dublin tomorrow. Myrna would be expecting me. Instead I'd be going to his funeral.

"It feels like some sort of joke. He was always playing jokes," Fran said.

I thought again of Nat's closed eyes and the impassiveness of his dead face. I could hear his voice in my ear. I remembered his views on women. I realised that I'd always been careful to keep him and Myrna in separate compartments of my life.

"Poor Daddy," Fran said in exactly the same way that Beth had said the words earlier and I realised that tears were running down my face.

FLOATING LIGHT BULBS

Beth and I flopped in her bedroom, two rag dolls with our thoughts floating over our heads in light bulb shapes the way they do in cartoons. We had come from burying her Dad in Mount Lawrence cemetery. It seemed like a fantasy. Any minute now Mr Page would stroll up the front path, put his key in the lock and life would click into motion once again. In the meantime our minds drifted only half-believing.

Beth's foremost thought: This is all a bad dream.

Fran's foremost thought: Maybe it didn't happen.

The funeral mass had been scary and sad. Organ music thundered over our heads. When the mass was finished crowds of people came shuffling up to shake Mrs Page's and Beth's hands. I sat with Josh, Alice and my father in the pew behind theirs. Beth huddled between her mother and grandmother. Her mother was pale and silent and pressed people's hands without speaking. Mrs Quill pulled each sympathiser towards her and yapped out things like: "Poor Winnie will never get over it," or, "I always said he drove too fast," as if she was a talking parrot. Beth kept her head down and twisted a hankie into bunny rabbits. When the girls from our class filed up wearing their uniforms I thought she was going to dive under the seat. There were so many wreaths and bouquets of flowers heaped around the coffin that the air smelt sweet and sickly.

"I still think Daddy will come back," Beth said to me, her voice coming out muffled and choked from the hollow of pillows on the other bed.

Once a woman turned up at her home after a gap of eight years. She had left an aeroplane during a stopover and lived in the woods, on the streets and in shelters in the intervening period. Then one day she remembered that she had invested some shares in a telephone company and decided to check them out. When she walked into the building and told them who she was the telephone people called her family and she was reunited with them.

I still hoped that sometime I'd look up and find my mother standing in front of me. I knew how Beth felt. There was no need for words.

Beth was wearing a black trouser suit. It made her look very small and unhappy. Even so, I hadn't seen her cry. Not in the church, or the graveyard. Now, even though her voice sounded heavy with tears, she stared dry-eyed at the overhead lampshade.

"I'm not going to cry because if I start I won't be able to stop," she'd said to me the night before at the hospital mortuary. We sat on wooden chairs against the walls while all sorts of people filed in past the open coffin and stared at Mr Page as if they'd never seen him before. I had stayed sitting along with Daddy, Beth and her mother and Mrs Quill. Some of Mr Page's relations turned up as well but even Daddy didn't know who they were. Before the coffin was closed Beth stepped forward very quickly and wiped a smear of lipstick off her dead father's forehead. A big woman with copper hair and tons of jewellery had pressed a gooey kiss on him as she filed passed. I had felt Beth beside me glow with hatred while her grandmother hissed. Her mother didn't seem to notice anything.

I was amazed at how alive Mr Page looked although he was

dead. I kept expecting him to sit up, wink at me, produce a pack of cards and say "Take one each, girls. Any card you like."

Now that the funeral was over it was hard to know how to pass the time. I wondered if Beth would like to change out of her black suit into jeans and a T-shirt and come down to the loft. Then I thought better of it. There was a memory of her father – not the one about him taking a pee – connected with the outhouse. It had just come into my mind. Maybe it was because it coincided with Lynda sending us a postcard that arrived the day before yesterday and this memory concerned both of them.

It had been two years ago. The Pages were having a Sunday lunchtime cocktail party and I had come to it with Daddy and Lynda. As soon as we got a chance Beth and I escaped to the loft with some vol-au-vents and orange juice. We were racing caterpillars we'd found in the garden on a sheet of white paper, which was a pretty senseless and boring thing to do, but also screamingly funny. We had little twigs to prod them with and mine had curled into a ball and wouldn't move.

Suddenly there were noises from down below. We looked through the trapdoor and saw Lynda race in then jump up and down, hugging herself and giggling. She was wearing a new yellow sundress with shoestring straps. She was really pleased with it because Auntie Theo told her she appeared as if she was ready to take a bath. I held my breath, sure that she was going to look up and see us, or climb the ladder herself. I peeped at Beth, but she was staring at something else. She had a better view of the entrance and saw her father before I did. As Mr Page stepped in after Lynda she reached out and pinched my arm.

The pair of them faced each other for a few seconds then Mr Page stepped up and put his arms right round Lynda and squeezed her close in a big hug. She went kind of limp, and giggled some more. Then she stopped because Mr Page kissed her. I held my breath waiting for her to cry out or hit him. Suddenly they began to tussle. I looked across and saw that Beth had crossed her fingers over her eyes and was peeping out through them. Mr Page was pushing Lynda back against the wall and Lynda was saying, "No, no. Stop now."

I squirmed, not knowing what to do. I felt terrible at being there. This was so embarrassing. My sister was acting crazy. Then, just as I thought I'd have to spring down like Batman coming to the rescue, Lynda did something that made Mr Page yell in agony and wriggled herself free. Once she was out of Mr Page's grasp she started saying he should keep to people his own age.

Mr Page doubled over as if he had a cramp and his breath came in quick gulps. When she saw that she got sorry and held out her hand and asked if he was all right, did he want her to bring him a glass of water.

"No," he said, when he got his breath back. "Come here," he said, stretching towards her. She stepped close enough for him to stroke her hair. "Oh you divil," he said. "If only I was twenty years younger you'd never get away with a trick like that."

In two seconds she was gone and he stood there, pulling a big white hankie out of his pocket to mop his face and the top of his bald head which was giving off a crimson glow.

Alice said there had been a girl in the car with Mr Page when he crashed. I couldn't ask Beth if it was true. Just thinking about it made me feel as shy as I became when people asked questions about my dead mother, or about Daddy's girlfriend.

The bedroom was a bit stuffy but if I suggested it Beth would probably say she didn't want to go to the loft. We'd hardly been there since my periods started. When I told Beth what had happened me she started saying silly things like, "Now you'll have boyfriends and you won't want to see me anymore". I didn't know any boys, and with Auntie Theo there I didn't think I ever would, unless it was one of Josh's weird friends. She also complained that I'd grown too large, she was only up to my shoulder, and she felt stupid walking beside me. Well, I felt stupid walking beside her too, but that was not going to make me break our friendship.

"You're a late developer, that's all," I said.

That made her even madder. I made her feel retarded. I made her feel like everyone in the world was looking at her and saying how slow she was.

"Fran?"

Her voice came from the other bed.

"What?"

"How do you fit four elephants into a Mini?"

"Two in the front. Two in the back."

"Smarty boots."

I gave her one: "How many elephants does it take to screw in a light bulb?"

"Daddy always gave people lifts," Beth said.

"So does mine."

"She was probably standing on the road, hoping someone would stop. He could never pass someone who looked as if they might desperately need a lift, especially girls or women. He was just making sure nothing bad happened to them."

"Sure," I said.

"Now, with your periods started, I suppose you'll be going off looking for men with cars," she said, sitting up and unzipping her black jacket.

"Stop being so stupid, Beth," I said.

"Two," she said. "It takes two elephants, but you need a real big bulb."

FLOATING LIGHT BULBS

The rumours began the evening after Nat Page's death. They percolated through the crowds who came to the removal of the body from the hospital mortuary to the Church of the Holy Rosary. It was hinted that agents from the office of the Revenue Commissioners had evidence that some of his financial dealings were decidedly shady. It was even claimed that some of the strangers who showed up at the ceremonies were not relatives but income-tax spies. When I was asked if I knew anything no warning bulb lit up inside my head. Nat was a wealthy man. He'd made most of his money through shrewd dealings and the high fees people paid him for advice about investments. I was glad to let him handle my own money matters from my early days in Limerick. The less I had to bother over accounts the more time I had for other business. Nat was the one who looked after that side of things.

"Come to your senses," I said to the first person that mentioned the stories. "You know Limerick people. That's just begrudgery. That's someone who didn't get on the bandwagon and now, when Nat is dead, wants to throw some mud at him."

I made the funeral arrangements, even though I found it very hard because it brought memories – the shock, the nastiness, the disbelief when Jane died – flooding back. Even so, I did everything I could: Church arrangements, choice of coffin, hotel for refreshments, buying the flowers, purchase of grave, things that Nat had done for me in my own calamity. I took one step at a time and hoped I wouldn't trip. Trouble on the business front was the last thing on my mind.

As I went through the motions of arranging his burial I recalled the first piece of advice I could remember him giving me. "Always bring a raincoat and £1.00." I felt a smile tug at my lips as I recalled him saying it. A raw country boy in a suit that was a size too small, working to impress myself and other callow schoolboys with his knowledge of women and the ways of the world.

The £1.00 was so you could bring her in someplace for tea and cakes. The raincoat was to spread on the ground afterwards when you'd found a good courting place. It was a typical Nat Page remark. Something that was kind of funny but offered to make you realise what a good sort he was, and that he knew how to get what he wanted. I kept the recollection, like a good deed in a naughty world, to cheer me up as I drove down to collect Winnie and Beth for the funeral mass.

After we'd laid him to rest the bubble burst. The rumours became reality. My progress to date as a successful professional man was cast in a different light.

In the 1970s most of the people in business or private practice had made a good deal of money. It was a time of opportunity for those who had a few quid to spare. Nat Page had an outstanding financial brain, going beyond orthodox investment practices and discovering all kinds of ways and means for his clients to make a little more interest here, a better rate of return there. I was happy to let him get on with it. When he suggested that he bank my money in our joint names it seemed like a good idea. I saw no need to keep a check on how things were going. I knew he'd tell me if there were any problems. The money was my retirement fund. Thanks to Nat I could look forward to an easeful old age.

"I've been trying to contact you, Mr Cleeve." The man behind the desk bent his fine crop of silver hair over a sheaf of papers with figures on it. Nat's chief accountant hovered at his shoulder, refusing to meet my eye. A large portrait of Nat's father-in-law bristled at us from the large gilt-framed portrait on the back wall. He was wearing his mayoral chain and rested his hand on a large leather-bound book.

"We've been making some investigations and your name has surfaced from time to time," said the silver-haired man.

"I don't see why that should be," I said.

"Well we ain't no geniuses, like your friend Mr Page," he said, "but it looks like you could be in a whole lot of trouble."

"Oh, I don't think so. I'm sure Nat left everything in order," I said. "I had complete trust in him."

"So I can see," said the man and added, "More fool you."

My temples began to pound.

"There is a difficulty," he gave me a sour look. "A great deal of money seems to have passed through the books, however, there are certain problems."

I was glad to hear it. The more problems these officious bastards had the better. I dabbed at my nostrils with a tissue and discovered I was starting a nosebleed.

"It seems that Mr Page expropriated large amounts of money that had been entrusted to him by various people. The bad news, Mr Cleeve, is that you were one of them. To put it bluntly, you've been robbed. The good news is that we can't bring charges against you because the money had been taken completely out of your control."

It took them some time to explain the details to me, but when they'd finished I could see the picture clearly enough. Nat had embezzled me. It was unbelievable. I couldn't take it in. I wanted to put my hands over my ears and block out the unwelcome truth.

"Did you know about this?" I challenged the chief accountant who leaned over the back of a chair looking as if he might at any minute disappear.

"I can't be held responsible," he said, addressing his twitching hands. "As a matter of fact I had already tendered my notice to the deceased. My connection with the firm is already broken. I am merely here to observe the formalities." He spoke in a low rapid voice as if he couldn't get shut of the whole affair fast enough.

I pressed my handkerchief against my nostrils, temples pounding worse than ever, feeling as if brains as well as blood were beginning to ooze out of my skull.

The silver-haired man made some more explanatory remarks but none of it made sense. As soon as I could I reeled from the office, my nose still spurting blood, my hankie a sodden rag. I felt I'd been mortally wounded. A man I recognised as the owner of a chain of local amusement arcades was sitting in the waiting room. He glanced at me with a mixture of fright and curiosity. "Is all our money gone?" he croaked.

I went down to the WC on the half-landing and splashed my face with water until my nosebleed finally stopped. Nat was a chancer. I'd always known that. But not with me. Not with his best friend's hard earned money. I couldn't believe that he'd deliberately defrauded me. There had to be some mistake. He'd always been on my side. He'd helped me to buy Riverview. He'd been there for me when Jane died. I'd gone through the recent days shaking people's hands in memory of him, running from pillar to post for Winnie, pinching myself now and then to make sure I wasn't dreaming and grieving all the time because I was going to miss him so much.

I lifted my head and looked into the small mirror over the basin, trying to focus on my face and see if I'd washed off all the blood. Instead, I saw Nat Page. He carried a raincoat over his arm. Then he put it down, took a £5.00 note out of my top

78

pocket and rubbed it on his shirt to build up a static charge. I knew what was going to happen next, but as always I was bemused.

He crumpled the fiver into a ball and placed it on his outstretched hand where it clung on as if glued there. Suddenly, it jumped to the back of his hand and as I watched closely crawled to the tip of his forefinger. Next I saw it float several inches above his hand. My eyes hurt from staring but I was determined not to blink, to keep my eye on the money.

"See," he said, as he turned his hand palm round and let the fiver land on his palm.

"Everything alright in there," someone was banging on the WC door.

"Just finished," I shouted as Nat smirked, unfolded the fiver and stepped forward to tuck it back into my pocket.

ANY CARD YOU LIKE

One of the problems with the three-card trick – as Beth confessed while I was shuffling the deck – was that she didn't quite know how it was done. We were good friends again, brought closer by her Dad's death. We spent most of our free time at the very end of her back garden, out of earshot of the house.

It was too hot and stuffy in the loft so we sat on tree stumps almost hidden by the heavy grass grown thick with buttercups and dandelions. Cascades of hawthorn tumbled over the back wall and elderflowers as big as saucers scented the air. A large gorse bush glittered against the end wall of the outhouse.

"Hearts, clubs, spades or diamonds. You can pick any two you like," Beth said.

I picked spades and clubs.

"OK, that leaves me with hearts and diamonds," Beth said.

The night the Titanic hit the iceberg a gambler had decided to stay up late to play cards. At the moment of impact he was holding the two of spades, the king of spades and the three of clubs. On their backs they carried a picture of the fluttering flag of the White Star line. He was one of the lucky ones who escaped in a rowing boat. Years later the complete pack, which he'd tucked into his pocket was auctioned in London. The person who bought it hoped to discover its winning secrets.

I wondered if there had been a pack of cards in Mr Page's pocket when he was killed. There usually was. It was her father who had shown Beth the mind-reading trick. One thing annoyed me – Beth was using his death as a weapon for getting her own way. I was supposed to fall in with all her plans. "You've got to let me choose what we're going to do," she'd say. If I tried to disagree she wailed that I was mean and selfish. "Alright," she'd say, "Go off and find someone your own size. Don't pick on me." If she hadn't been my best friend I'd have stayed away until she stopped being so horrible.

"Fran. Fran, you're not listening. You took spades and clubs out, so that leaves hearts and diamonds. Which do you want to choose a card from?"

"Hearts," I said.

"Ok, that means diamonds are gone. Now decide what numbers you want, two to eight, or nine to ace."

"Two to eight," I said. The trick seemed to be working. I was hopelessly confused.

"Fine," Beth said, "Keep those numbers fixed in your mind."

She looked at me over the fanned out pack. "I'm going to get my ears pierced," she said.

My brother Josh had just had his right nostril pierced. When Daddy asked him how he expected to get a decent job with that yoke on his face he said he didn't plan to work anywhere but in radio or television and pierced nostrils were all the fashion.

"Fran!" When Beth was angry her face turned pink.

I was glad to keep anything in my mind that kept me from worrying about Auntie Theo. She was nastier than ever these days. Daddy was at home, but he usually ate his meals in a restaurant. She blamed me for keeping him away when she'd gone to the trouble of making a nourishing stew, or cooking rice pudding. I wished that I could eat someplace else. Her stews were full of grease and her rice pudding was slop. I sat opposite her shoving the goo into my mouth and trying not to think of awful stuff like snot and phlegm.

"Wilful waste makes woeful want," she'd say.

"Who's going to provide for us when your father has sold the roof over our heads. That's what I want to know?" she'd said today out of the blue before dropping a gobbet of unasked for jam on my rice where it looked exactly like a clot of blood.

I never paid attention when she talked in riddles, but this wasn't a riddle. It sounded like something peculiar was going on. Maybe she was going crazy.

"So, which card will you take?" Beth asked shaking them inches away from my face.

I thought of my two of spades and three of clubs and the gambler on the Titanic. "The king," I said.

"You can't have the king, you chose two to eight. It must be one of them," she said.

"Five," I said.

"Now you have five to eight. I have two to four," she grinned.

"Ok." I was really getting bored. Watching Beth's narrow fingers fiddling with the cards I grew bewildered and restless. Auntie Theo couldn't have been serious about Daddy selling Riverview. That would be disastrous. Where would I live?

"Which of my cards do you want?" Beth's eyes crinkled the way Mr Page's did and went all shiny when she was excited. Then her face grew angry again. "Hey! You're not with me." She glared.

"Give me the four," I said.

"Hey, now we have the two and three left. Which one do you want?"

The sun was shining but where we sat was overgrown and shady. "Do you know how to break a thread in a sealed bottle?" I asked. (You stood it in bright sunlight and used a magnifying glass to concentrate the sun's rays until the thread burned through.)

"No and I don't want to know. Tell me what number."

"Two," I said. "Two, two, two, two, two."

"So we remove the two and that leaves us with the three." She looked triumphant.

"I'm baking hot," I said.

I thought of how tired Daddy had looked this morning. He was talking on the telephone in the hall. His head was bent over the receiver and he was saying things like: "So what would you advise – that's right, six bedrooms". Riverview had six bedrooms Auntie Theo slept in the one off the half landing at the top of the first flight of stairs. "Sell the roof over our heads," she'd said.

"Fran!" Beth screamed.

According to Auntie Theo cards were the devil's game. You should always look at a card player's feet. Very often you'd find that they weren't feet at all, they were hooves. Beth had kicked off her sandals. Earlier, before we came out here, we'd painted our toenails with blue nail-polish so dark that it was almost black. Her toenails, as she hunched herself on the tree stump, one of two we'd carted up here during the winter to use as seats, looked as if they belonged to a monkey.

"So, abracadabra," Beth gave a huge sigh and waved her arms in a circle like a druid or something. "I am about to produce the card you left me which is the three of – ?"

"Clubs," I said.

"Not clubs. Hearts. You chose spades and clubs. I chose hearts and diamonds."

Midges had started to bite. I scratched my legs.

"I think I might become a magician if I don't become a stunt woman," Beth said.

I pushed away the recollection of Daddy saying to Josh, when they were arguing about his pierced nose, "It's time you started acting like an adult. You're a walking mess. Things are bad enough without having a hippy son."

"There aren't hippies anymore," Josh said. "And if you're talking about messes I heard in the broadcasting studio about the mess Mr Page left." Daddy looked at him as if he was a monster, then said in a dry voice, "Thanks."

The midge bites hurt as badly as the wallops Auntie Theo used to give me. It was good that I was too big for her to beat me anymore. The wooden spoon stayed in its jar. The last time she'd raised a hand to me was after the teapot and summer bazaar fiasco. That thing she'd said about 'the roof over our heads' had been to get me upset. She was a professional mental torturer. When I was little she'd threatened me with the Invisible Man, and a creature called Hairy Molly, and the Beast that lived in the cave behind the laurel hedge. More recently it was jibes at me for driving my father from the house or causing Mummy's death. I did my best to ignore her. I pretended that Mummy was standing behind her, listening to it all, and looking at me so kindly that I melted with love and adoration for her. She had also started belittling Beth: "I don't know why you hang around with that wizened little creature, surely, Francesca, you could find a proper friend. That girl has a want. It's written all over her." And "She has a cuteness about her that she got straight from her father." And "You'd think her mother would buy her some proper girl clothes." (This was unfair. Beth's wardrobe was crammed with pretty dresses bought by her mother. Dresses that made Beth wail in horror. Dresses you wouldn't be seen dead in. Dresses that were dresses that were dresses that would make you a laughing stock.)

The effect of all this criticism was to make me more determined than ever that nothing in the whole world would stop Beth from being my friend. Even if she was acting strange, refusing to come in to look at the shops, or even to play tennis in Riverview, or come to guide meetings.

"You go, Big Shot," she'd say and looking at her thin freckled face, and seeing the shadows under her eyes, and remembering Auntie Theo's scorn I couldn't leave her.

"You're miles away. You're not with me at all," All the playing cards scattered around me on the ground as she jumped to her feet and threw the pack at me.

"Sorry, sorry." In my desire to appease her I put my hand down right on top of a nasty briar. The thorns ripped into the palm of my hand and I cried out in pain but Beth took no notice.

"Feck off, Fran. You're useless. You're no fun anymore. She fumbled at the back pocket of her combat pants. They were fashionably baggy and I wished that I had a pair myself.

"The trick is over. It's too late," she said.

My hand was hurting like hell.

"I was listening," I said trying to blot out the soreness.

"Oh shit," said Beth. "It's hopeless. I'd been doing it all wrong anyway." She began to cry.

"It's only a silly old trick," I said.

"It was Daddy's trick. He tried time and time again to show me. I've let him down. I hate myself," she said.

I thought of how he'd vanished, like a true trickster, leaving nothing behind him but a puff of smoke. "Maybe if you practised a bit more," I said removing my hand from under my bottom where I'd placed it to ease the stinging. A nasty pink weal stretched from my wrist to my third finger.

Beth reached down and the next thing I knew she'd hurled a clod of damp earth at me that landed on my clean white T-shirt. I looked down at my dirty chest in dismay. If Auntie Theo caught me coming home in this state I wouldn't be let out again for a week.

"Serves you right." Beth gave me an evil grin.

"My hand is all scratched," I said. I bowed my head, not wanting to let her see I was smarting.

Then she said, "Something's happening, Fran. I'm scared."

"Like what," I asked, brushing at my front with my good hand.

"People ringing the house. Mummy saying we'll have to go away. I don't know what it's about. It's all started since Daddy died. I answered the phone yesterday. It was a woman who started to cry and say Daddy was a huckster, he'd taken everything her husband owned."

"She must have been nuts," I said.

"Has your father said anything?" she asked. "I mean anything about Daddy."

"He cried at the funeral," I said. "He was so sorry it had happened."

"Mummy says your parents and mine were a foursome," Beth said. "That's why we have to stand up for each other through thick and thin. Swear, Fran."

I had to use my left hand to swear because my right one felt as if it was on fire.

"And if you hear anything you'll let me know," she said.

"All I ever hear is Auntie Theo," I said. "And all she goes on about is . . ." I remembered all the horrible things she'd started saying about Beth.

"Is what?" Beth stared at me intently.

"Is . . . is . . ." I racked my brains. "The good food she cooks, her rice pudding, what . . . what's going to happen to us when Daddy sells the roof over our heads."

"I see," Beth's face sort of folded up, the way the cards did, gathering in their secrets. "I see," she repeated. She gave me a sharp look. "You swore, Fran. Through thick and thin, whatever happens. You swore. The crazy woman on the phone last night said she was losing her house because my father was a two-timing huckster. She said that there were men with folding tables at Listowel Races playing Find the Lady and they were honest men compared to him."

"Daddy isn't really selling our house," I said. I refused to believe there was any question of him doing so. My throat felt dry. I needed a cool glass of water. Perspiration was running down my face.

Suddenly Beth got off her log and knelt beside me and impulsively kissed me on the cheek. It was as if she was sorry for me and couldn't think of anything to say.

It was time for me to go home. There was my maths still to be done, and an essay for history class. But I was reluctant to move. Suddenly I didn't care about the midge bites or my scratched hand or Beth insisting on having her own way. I wanted to stay here in the deep shade. I listened to the twittering birds and the soft sound of Beth breathing, like some small animal.

"Maybe I'll build myself a tree house right here," I said. "You could come down some nights and sleep over. I'd be like Robinson Crusoe. It'd be better than living with Auntie Theo. You could bring me out food."

In some deep part of me I thought that if Daddy ever did sell our house Beth would ask her mother if I could move in and live with them. I'd only be one extra person. Their house was nearly as big as ours. The idea seemed exciting even though I'd have to put up with Mrs Quill's remarks. Beth's grandmother called me a poor little wretch. "Is this the one whose poor mother . . ." she'd begin, then stare at me until her eyes swam behind her glasses. I could stand that. Mrs Quill would be on my side. I wouldn't be disturbing anyone. As it was, I often slept in the second bed in Beth's room.

"Spain," Beth was saying. "I don't want to. I'd hate it. I'm not going to go."

I propped my back against a tree trunk. My hand felt much better. I'd plucked a dock leaf and placed it over the cut like you do with nettle stings. "Mmmh!" I said. I had no idea what she was talking about. "Mmmh!"

ANY CARD YOU WANT

"Never give a sucker an even break." That's a quotation from Nat Page's commonplace book.

I once saw him take on a bony-faced fellow with wild white hair, dressed up in a threadbare grey suit over a woollen cardigan, and a blue shirt with a worn collar, at the horse fair on Spancill Hill. The man was laying down cards on a coloured cloth spread on a folding table. A crowd of sullen faced youngsters clustered around him, egging each other on to have a go.

Nat strolled over to where they stood nudging and jostling and staring at the dingy cards and the man's restless, shifting hands.

"Any card you want," said the cardsharp.

The urchins gaped at the tenner Nat threw down on the table. £1.00 was the usual bet.

"Any card you want," the man repeated, "All above board. Pick any one you like," he turned them over to show us the queen, a seven, and a ten. His eyes flickered even faster than his nimble hands, as he watched out for approaching gardai.

I looked at Nat. His expression had grown mean and jubilant, the way it did when he was out to expose an opponent's weakness, or make a killing. He moved in on the little table. Seconds later the huckster was counting out money into his hand.

"Leave it, Nat," I said.

"One more go," he said, without raising his head. The cluster of shabbily dressed urchins, as they closed in around us, gave out a smell like that of puppies, but with a sweatier undertone. I thought of saving myself, of running away; but like them I was hooked.

"There's nothing random about it," Nat said a short while later tucking the wad of filthy notes into an inside pocket as the man folded up his table and skulked off, his tail between his legs, saying that the guards had spotted him. He'd be prosecuted if caught.

"Hey mister, give us some money," the biggest of the boys said while the rest stared at Nat admiringly.

Nat ignored him as he patted the bulge of banknotes above his heart.

"Hey mister! Hey mister!"

As we walked away from the noisy chorus I felt like an accomplice who had helped to rob a beggar.

"How much did you win?" I asked.

"I forget," Nat said.

After he died I wondered if he could have put a figure on the amount of money he'd tricked me out of. A couple of hundred! People like Nat didn't bother adding on noughts. People like Nat thought that everybody was fair game. But there was no point in being bitter. I had too much to do. First of all I was going to have to get rid of the house.

"I've found you a jewel," Nat said when he first told me that Riverview was for sale privately. I thought owning a Georgian mansion would protect me financially, but now I discovered it had turned into a liability. I needed ready money to pay the house insurance, heating bills, telephone bills, maintenance – the roof had begun to leak. And in the space of a week the washing machine, tumbler drier, and refrigerator packed up and a major crack appeared in the top of the kitchen range.

"This happens when all these things are bought at the same time. It's called built-in obsolescence," the electrical dealer said. "Usually people buy major appliances one at a time."

I decided that we could make do with just buying a

refrigerator. The family could wash their clothes themselves. I'd bring mine to the launderette.

"You're not going to find it easy to sell. Every big house in the city is on the market," the bank manager advised. I'd called in about increasing my overdraft. "What people are looking for now is small. Town houses. Those mews houses you built out behind your place would fetch more than the house itself today. You should have held onto them."

"Thanks," I said. That was all the help he gave me.

Then there was Theo. She was homeless. Her relations had forgotten about her after she came to Limerick. I counted up the number of years she'd been living in Riverview and was horrified. It had only been a temporary arrangement.

On the second Sunday after Nat's death I held a conference with my children. I chose a Sunday because I could be sure that Theo would have gone to church. We sat in the front room around the pedestal table, with mugs of tea and coffee. It seemed a pity that Lynda wasn't with us. I missed her. She was the sunniest of them all. I was still puzzled as to the reasons for her absence; except for the fact that there was something romantic about it. Well, good luck to her, I thought. She wasn't any younger than her mother had been when she took up with me. But I pushed away the memory of the dark-haired young woman who'd once told me my fortune. It hurt too much.

I tried to be as objective and businesslike as possible as I spoke to the children. I explained to Alice, Josh and Fran that I was in a tight spot. No money. Not much work coming in. It was up to them to decide whether they wanted to move out and live separately or stay together.

"I'm getting a flat with Mark," Alice said immediately as if it was the most natural thing in the world. I wondered how she was going to square it with Theo, but that was her own affair.

"I can't stop you," I said. "You're over 21."

"What's going to happen to you, Dad?" Josh asked and I almost forgave him for the faddish monstrosity glittering at the edge of his nostril.

I studied the beautiful mottled surface of the polished table and heard the gate of the past slamming behind me.

"I have no idea," I said. The self of the 1970s who'd once slipped so eagerly into this Georgian house thanks to Nat Page had vanished in the twinkling of an eye. All that was left of him was a man in his 50s with egg on his face.

I'd got above myself with my imposing residence. It was a historical relic of the decades of early nineteenth-century prosperity enjoyed by the few, while the indigenous population, my own people, suffered from famine, evictions, and forced emigration. Who had I imagined myself to be aping – old Smyth-Drummond? No wonder my family had broken off all contact with me. No wonder Jane had been unhappy.

"If your great-grandaddy could see you now," Nat Page said, grinning, the day I signed the contract to buy Riverview.

"It's too big," was the first thing Jane said when I brought her to see it. "The whole idea was to get us a good modern house," was the next thing she said.

"I'll look after everything," I said. "All you need to do is feed Francesca and rest. The bigger ones can mind themselves and the new help seems a nice girl."

"I'm telling you I won't be able to cope, although you don't care I suppose." She scowled at the solid walls turning pale gold in the evening sun. She was being difficult. Lately, no matter what I did she turned my motives around and accused me of being inconsiderate.

"I thought you'd love it, because I certainly do," I said.

"You," she said. "What would you know about it?"

I felt myself growing angry. I was not a dragon, not a monster, neither male chauvinist nor pig. I worshipped Jane. She was my reality, the beloved sweetheart, all I wanted. Everything I did was to show her how deeply she was loved.

"I know we need a decent house," I said. "And we won't find anything to beat this."

I refused to believe otherwise during the weeks in which we moved out of the ex-orphanage and in here. The gynaecologist casually mentioned the moodiness of post-natal women and how it could usually be cured by a holiday or a piece of jewellery. I bought her pearls, I made plans for a surprise trip. I'd have given her the moon. Then, after she hanged herself, I kept Riverview on as some sort of secure base for my motherless children. It was the only thing I could do for them.

"What's going to happen about Auntie Theo?" Fran didn't look at me but stirred her cup of coffee.

"I don't know," I said.

"There are some nice *small* houses being built just down by the triangle," Alice said to me. "She and Fran would fit into one of them very nicely. What do you think of that, Daddy?"

I didn't think anything except that the houses she mentioned were way beyond my present means.

"Well," I said. "We don't have to make up our minds about anything right away. The first thing we have to do is get rid of this place."

"Does that mean we're poor?" Fran asked in a nervous voice.

"Poor but fairly honest." I managed a laugh.

THE SIGNED BULLET

I felt as if I was the innocent victim of a plot and had been condemned to face a firing squad. I looked at the three sitting at the table. Alice looking sneaky and satisfied, Josh tilting his chair and drumming the table top with his bony fingers and refusing to meet my gaze, Daddy acting all hot and bothered. I hurt all over. It didn't seem fair that my life could be disposed of just like that. Being dumped with nobody but Auntie Theo would be awful beyond belief. All I could think of to say was: "What about Dusty?"

"Oh, I want to do the best for everybody – including Dusty," Daddy said.

"At least there won't be any grass to cut if you buy one of those places. They have no gardens," Josh said as if he was a property expert. He was supposed to mow the lawns in Riverview but he never did. Every year we ended up having to get in a man with a scythe.

"Actually, I'm probably going to live in the Page's house," I said, thinking fast. "Beth has asked me. Her mother and her granny agree it would be nice for both of us." I hadn't seen Beth for a couple of days, but I had given the matter of moving in with her some thought. I could easily have the spare bed in her room. Mrs Page even called it "Fran's bed" I'd used it so often. If I begged her she'd have to take me in.

Alice pushed her hair back from her face and studied me. "Don't be daft," she said. "Anyway, you're still a child. You need Auntie Theo to keep you in order and she can't be expected to go off and live on her own after taking care of you all these years."

I was so furious that I clenched my fists and moved towards her to give her a punch.

"See what I mean?" Alice spoke to Daddy. "She's a little wild cat."

"Hold on a minute," Daddy said. "Simmer down, Fran. There's nothing fixed yet. And I'm certainly not buying one of those houses, Josh, thank you very much. For a start, I can't afford to. Plus, they're not worth the money."

"You wouldn't mind if I lived with the Pages, would you Daddy? I wouldn't be any bother to them. I promise," I said.

Suddenly he looked as if he was about to be shot. He stared deeply into my eyes and his face seemed to grow very still. When he raised his hand to stroke his chin I saw it was shaking.

"I'm afraid that's out of the question," he said, his voice heavy and slow.

"Even if Mrs Page came and asked you herself?" My eyes had started to water.

"Stop being such a fusspot," Alice said. "Daddy hasn't even sold this house yet. There's nothing arranged. Didn't you hear him say so, dopey?"

I suspected that she was setting a trap to catch me. "If poor Mummy was here she wouldn't let you do this," I yelled, then, somehow, I stumbled from the room and ran out into the back yard making sure to slam the outside door hard as I went. All my family were unbearable. Alice was pure nasty, Josh a weirdo, even Daddy didn't want me to be happy, and Lynda was gone. I stood gazing at the grey paving stones. A long shudder went through me from head to toe as Dusty came slinking from the outhouse to flop at my feet. Horrible thoughts were shooting through my head. If they left me with Auntie Theo I'd never speak to any of them again.

With Dusty trailing me I threw myself down on the grassy patch behind the wire netting that screened off our tennis court. I propped my back against the old cherry tree and wished I had never been born. The spiky leaves of the palms rattled in a light breeze. Pigeons cooed in the copper beech. I froze as Auntie Theo advanced along the path by the side of the house. She didn't notice me. I could see shapes of the others through the kitchen window. I picked up a large stone and balanced it in my hand. If any of them came near me I'd let them have it straight between the eyes.

When nobody did come out I began to pluck at the frayed ends of my jeans. Auntie Theo was the only person who had been to church. Daddy had even kept us from mass. Our family were losing their religion. I blamed him for that as well as for everything else, especially as Mummy had loved our church so much that she'd joined it. Auntie Theo said it was a sign of weakness, and was probably the reason she'd committed suicide, which was more proof of her repulsiveness. I began to shiver. It was only when she was in her worst kind of temper that she said things as cruel as that. Next time I'd kill her. People like Auntie Theo shouldn't be allowed to live.

> *Oh beloved mother of mine*
> *I think about you all the time.*
> *I would never have let you die.*
> *We will be together someday.*
> *This is not "goodbye."*

Suddenly, I saw Mummy hovering like a shadow, a filled space, at the corner of my vision. Although I knew how she had died I saw she was bleeding from self-inflicted bullet wounds. Then she stepped towards me and removed a small object from between her lips and held it out. It had her name, "Jane Smyth-Drummond" engraved on it.

I balanced it on the palm of my hand. I stretched out one leg, then the other and rolled the small pellet against my jeans. "I must be gone, darling, Fran," my mother whispered then vanished into the ancient branches of the cherry tree. I felt as lonely as I'd ever been in my life. My future pressed up against my vision like a stone wall, a hopeless dead end. The dust blew into my throat. I could do nothing but bash my head against the hard surface until my brains turned to pulp and I didn't care what happened. I was doomed. This was my lot. I rocked myself gently, tossing the signed bullet in the air again and again.

"What are you doing, Fran?" Daddy came round the corner from the yard.

"Nothing. Playing jacks," I said, tossing the pebble up again and catching it on the back of my hand.

"The truth of the matter is, Fran, we're going to have to bite the bullet." Daddy had hunkered down beside me. He looked awkward and uncomfortable.

"I want to live with you, not with Auntie Theo?" I said.

"Look," he said, "I don't know what I'm going to do. How I'm going to manage."

A fine breeze blew across the garden and a blossom floated down onto my lap like a false promise.

THE SIGNED BULLET

It was only days since Nat's death, but it seemed as if a lifetime had passed. I was in dire straits. I had a welter of ideas about disposing of Riverview, closing the Limerick office and heading for Dublin where, with any luck, I would make some definite arrangement about permanent accommodation in Myrna's hotel. It was a relief to know that my older children were making their own plans. Even Lynda had sent letters from London with news of sharing a flat with a number of other people and details of various amusing and unusual jobs – such as walking peoples' dogs and working in a bingo hall.

I pieced together a sort of explanation of why she had gone away – a boy, a misunderstanding, some sort of rumpus in Riverview, Theo playing the heavy aunt.

The bullet arrived by post inside a letter signed by the owners of the building where I had my Dublin office. They suggested that it might have escaped my notice that the lease was up. They were writing to inform me that the building had been sold and if I wished to retain occupancy I must negotiate terms with the new owners. They named a well-known speculator who had made his fortune by buying large premises and letting them to government agencies. My office consisted of one room and an ante-room. I knew it would be an unwanted black spot to the new landlords. It looked as if my hopes of continuing to practise in Dublin were doomed. I reluctantly faced the fact that business had fallen off up there even more than in Limerick. I'd have a better chance of getting new work if I opened a branch office at the North Pole. This meant that there was no point in continuing to stay in Myrna's place. I hadn't spoken to her since Nat's death. She must be wondering what had become of me.

Because of my close friendship with Nat I was looked upon as party to the skullduggery that had brought everyone to their knees.

"Sure weren't the two of you thick as thieves!" was the general opinion.

The streets of Limerick became full of people who wanted to buttonhole me and give me a piece of their mind. There were reports that I, too, had money salted away. Plus, they pointed out, I had Riverview. One of the grandest houses left standing in the city and I'd got it for a song. I'd be able to sell. It was worth ten times what I'd paid the poor alcoholic widow for it. There was only the slight matter of getting people interested and Bob's your uncle.

Walking from my car to the office began to remind me of stories my grandmother had told of running the gauntlet of snipers in O'Connell Street, Dublin, in the days of the Civil War. She died when I was seven. She'd been a Free Stater and hatred of DeValera and anything pertaining to him, or republicanism, was a compulsory ingredient of family life. "Your grandmother would have died of shame," my mother said when I told her who I planned to marry. She would also have poured scorn on my association with Nat Page. His people had fought on the other side in the Civil War. The aunt who paid for his education was a believer in a 32 county republic, a widow whose proud boast was that her husband had died from wounds received while taking part in an IRA ambush in which a Black and Tan officer and the young daughter of an Anglo-Irish family were killed.

My own interest in politics was negligible. Besides, nowadays so much was happening in the North I felt that ordinary people like myself only saw the tip of the iceberg. The country was in the grip of forces over which I had no control. I wasn't even able to look after my own business affairs, never mind the Irish Nation's. I'd been gulled into thinking that the world owed me a comfortable life.

As the days passed I began to experience shame and a sense of failure. And it became painfully clear, after another interview with my bank manager, how successfully Nat Page had pulled the wool over my eyes.

"His dying made no difference," I was told. "He'd bought himself a fine villa in the south of Spain. He'd already started to move all his assets out of the country."

I felt like a foolish woman who discovers, on her husband's death, that she was only a shadow. His real family, the people he truly cared about, lived somewhere else.

I'd been a sucker. Nat had turned into a Judas figure. All his schemes and plans for the future had had nobody but himself in mind.

I thought of Fran asking if she could go and live in the Page household. No way. Besides, it was being said that Winnie was heading off for Spain with all the loot and nobody could stop her.

I began to have imaginary conversations with Nat's ghost.

I cursed him for having escaped me.

I imagined what I would do if I got my hands on some of my lost funds.

I considered driving round to Winnie Page's house wearing a balaclava and robbing her. I knew where Nat kept his safe. He'd always kept a large amount of cash in the house.

I saw myself going berserk and raping Winnie because my life was ruined. She must have known what was going on.

I thought about what to do with Fran. Maybe Winnie had suggested that she move into the house like a charity child. It was a flagrant insult. She knew as well as I did that she owed me my money. Yesterday I'd seen her run into Todd's store like a frightened rabbit to avoid passing me in the street. Next time I'd follow her and spit in her face.

I turned to Alice for a little sanity. She was the oldest after all. I needed her to advise me about Fran – maybe she could stay in a hostel or a boarding-school for the next few crucial months, any place where she would have companionship and security while I sorted out my affairs.

"I was never let go to boarding school not even when Mummy died. I really think it would be best for her and Auntie Theo to stay together," Alice said. She sounded so grown-up and reasonable that I was inclined to agree.

Meanwhile, I brought an auctioneer out to look over the house with me. Checking it out with a view to selling I was shocked to find how badly the building had deteriorated. The plumbing was slum standard. All the tap washers in the bathroom were worn. The cistern of the downstairs lavatory had a serious leak. The boiler in the boiler house was on its last legs.

"You'll be lucky to get anything in the region of two hundred thou," the man said taking a penknife to the crumbling timber in the window frames. I'd been deluding myself about my desirable residence. It was in a bad way.

"I suppose you found it hard to stay committed to the place with the wife dead," he said.

I ignored his sidelong glance.

"One of Nat's victims has landed himself in double-trouble," he said. "He was caught trying to set his furniture shop on fire to get the insurance money. The queer thing is my only memory of Nat Page is of him lending me money one day when I met up with him by chance in Dublin after I'd had my pocket picked. You could ask one of your own for that kind of help and they wouldn't do anything for you." He folded his arms and stared at an unwieldy radiator. "Those yokes are a bit out of date," he said.

The pickpocket anecdote brought back Nat with his grey, sharpshooter's gaze.

"Did you ever pay the money back?" I asked.

He hooted with amusement. "Begob now that you mention it I never did. How about that?"

I wasn't surprised. He was a notorious scrounger. The only reason I was doing business with him was because he was the only estate agent who'd seemed interested in handling the sale. The others made excuses about staff shortages, a poor property market, and lack of interest in big old houses.

"Your man, Nat Page," he said as I saw him off the premises. "He's laughing, wherever he is, at the muddle he's left behind him. All he ever wanted to do was put a spanner in the works of as many wealthy Limerick people as possible. It was because he was jeered for his lack of background. He was blackballed from all the decent clubs when he came here first. He was never the type we wanted. They didn't even want him in the Men's Confraternity. The only reason he was ever let in anywhere was because of who his father-in-law was."

"I never knew that," I said, "and I knew him since we were in school together."

"A cute hawk," the auctioneer said.

I thought back to my first day in Limerick. Nat Page bouncing into my office. "Well, well, well – my old school pal, Henry. It's a small world."

"How did you know I was here?" I'd asked.

He looked me over closely and then he grinned.

"You're a marked man," he said sizing me up.

Maybe he'd been gunning for me all the time. Uneasily I saw myself caught out in sniper's territory and Nat Page crouched undercover, getting me into his sights.

WILLIAM TELL

I became extra careful. I wanted to be sure that I wasn't left to Auntie Theo's tender mercies.

"Now that your father has squandered away everything we are the ones expected to pay the price," she said sawing at the loaf of bread as if she was beheading an infidel.

She had on a dark blouse with a white collar and her hair stood up in all directions around her purple face. Cigarette smoke spiralled from a flowered china saucer. She was in a bad mood so I didn't argue with her. I'd rather argue with an elephant on the rampage. My chief aim was to attract as little of her attention as possible.

I'd had a dream in which she and I were being urinated on by a big black dog. I looked up the meaning in my dream book and discovered that a dog indicated a protector. As for urine – the Greeks recognised this as one of the most powerful symbols of the gathering of creative powers. My own feelings on waking had been disgust and fear, but maybe the book told the truth. I'd taken it from the bookcase in Lynda's abandoned room.

In another dream I was lined up against a wall while Daddy and the others took pot shots at me.

When Beth telephoned and asked me to come round to her house and stay for supper I slipped out without asking Auntie

Theo if I could go. Her mother was making a prawn curry. She had news to tell me. It was a big surprise. "A nice surprise," she added. Her words filled me with hope. She hadn't been back at school since her father died and I hadn't called round since the day we sat in the garden doing card tricks. I thought it better to hang around Riverview just in case everyone disappeared while my back was turned.

As I walked along the summery road I became certain that the surprise was going to be an invitation to move into the Page's house. I skipped a little and sang a few lines of, "*We all live in a yellow submarine*" as I thought of all the lovely things we could do if Mrs Page let me come and live with Beth.

I was also glad to get out of Riverview because Billy Kelly was fixing the door on the half-landing. Josh had thrown one of his shoes upstairs ahead of him and it smashed through the glass. Billy kept blessing himself and saying stupid things like, "Oh Sacred Heart of Jesus have mercy on a poor sinner", or "Sweet divine Mother of God protect us all", when Auntie Theo came up and had to step over the mess of broken glass, putty and sprigs of wood spread on an old newspaper to get to her own bedroom.

"There's no need for that sort of foolish carry on," she snapped.

"Sure what harm does it do," Billy said then began to hum "*Faith of our fathers*," as he thumbed fresh putty into place, delighted that he had vexed her.

Beth and her mother were in their big kitchen with all its shiny gadgets and fittings. It was much nicer than ours. I'd never mind doing any sort of cleaning here. A mouth-watering spicy smell hung in the air. A bag of rice and a saucer of sliced lemons were on the worktop. The large table was laden down with objects – big oil paintings of poultry, dogs and other domestic animals that had hung in their dining room were propped against the unlit Aga. Mrs Page was tearing up out-of-date Irish Racing Calendars and stuffing them into a plastic sack.

"Fran – there you are!" She sounded really pleased to see me.

"These go back to the year dot," she said. "Beth's grandad bought one every year. They were his bible."

"We're sorting out what we're going to sell," Beth said as she handed me a glass of Coca-Cola. I let one of the ice cubes slip into my mouth and pressed its coldness against my palate while I waited for her to explain.

"Mosquito spray," Mrs Page had finished with the old calendars and was now taking things out of a high cupboard. "We might need that." She put the tiny bottle to one side.

"For Spain," Beth said. She plucked a pink rose from a vase and tucked it behind her left ear and giggled wildly. I failed to see the joke.

"You should just see your face, Fran," she said and giggled harder than ever.

I wondered if her daddy's sudden death had affected her brain. I thought of what she'd said about nasty phone calls. Maybe she'd imagined them. Maybe Auntie Theo was right about her being strange. Then I thought about how my own daddy was saying he was poor. Something funny was going on. Whatever it was Beth wasn't upset as she added some old Beano annuals to the sackful of Racing Calendars. She was jubilant.

"I suppose you're wondering what all this is, Fran" she waved an arm at the opened cupboards, the things stacked on chairs, the folded clothes on the ironing board.

"It looks like you're spring cleaning," I said.

"Much, much more exciting. Mummy and I are going to go and live in Marbella, in a fantastic villa!" she said, "And Granny is coming as well. Daddy bought the place a few years ago. I'll show you pictures of it after we've eaten".

I began to feel intensely suspicious.

"What's wrong? You're looking at me as if I have two heads." There was something gleefully unkind in the way she was carrying on.

"I don't understand," I said.

"You can come out in the holidays if you want to. It'll be fun. Can't she Mummy?"

"Is this really true?" I asked. My heart was beating violently.

"Of course it's true," Beth said. "Cross my heart."

"You never told me."

"You weren't listening. I was doing the any card you want trick. Remember?"

I looked past her out of the kitchen window. I could see the loft's roof. It looked ready to fall down. Since Mr Page's death, the world kept breaking up into a thousand pieces, but at least Beth was there.

"I was listening," I said. "I promised and so did you that we'd always help each other." I couldn't trust myself to say any more. The place where the briar scratched my hand was still tender. I pressed my fingertips into it to make it hurt more. It reassured me that I hadn't imagined our bond. She couldn't go off and leave me at Auntie Theo's mercy. She was my closest friend.

She was just teasing, putting on an act. I remembered Mr Page, when we were very small, reaching behind our ears and producing coins he then gave us to spend in the shop. But now he was dead. He couldn't magic houses in Spain out of nowhere. Daddy said there wasn't any money around.

"It's really glamorous", Beth babbled on. "Lot's of famous people live there. I can't wait. You should see the balcony – flowers all over it. And there's a pool. And tennis courts, proper ones, proper grass ones".

"Joke's over," I said. "You've forgotten that I was supposed to be coming to live with you." I looked from Beth to her mother. Mrs Page had a watchful expression on her face.

"Who told you that, Fran?" she asked.

"My daddy thinks it would be a good idea," I bluffed. "You see he's having to sell our house so there's no place for me."

I was surprised at the way colour rushed into Mrs Page's cheeks.

"Oh my dear," she said. "You mustn't blame Beth's father. He was doing his best for everyone."

I felt as if something had exploded then I saw the whole thing so clearly that I was dazzled. I was like someone who has had a blindfold removed and finds the world lit up by a searchlight. Mr Page had stolen Daddy's money and Mrs Page was as wicked and deceitful as he had been. She wasn't going to give it back.

"You stole Daddy's money, didn't you? That's how you're able to go away and live someplace else," I said.

"What a thing to say," gasped Mrs Page.

"You haven't denied it. You can't." Rage and hurt made me reckless. "You're all thieves and liars," I shouted.

Mrs Page had crossed over to the large pine dresser. When I shouted "thieves and liars", the drawer she was pulling open came right out and the sound of cutlery clattering on tiles echoed through the kitchen.

"Damn," she said in a loud voice.

Beth rushed over and between them they scooped the shiny pieces from the ground and dropped them back into their compartments.

"It's alright Mummy. It was an accident," Beth crooned as Mrs Page muttered and moaned.

The sun was beginning to set and shafts of light gave a satiny sheen to the red-tiled floor. They both reached for the same fork and bumped heads. As they straightened up they looked at each other like conspirators. I was getting the old ball of twine pain in my tummy. But this time it was more like an arrow. I could feel its feathered shaft shaking from the impact as it protruded from my groin.

"Why did you ask me over, Beth?" I asked. "Is it because you think you're so great?"

Beth jumped to her feet. "Um, well, Fran, just get yourself out of here this minute." She looked at me fiercely. Auntie Theo was right about her being small and wizened. "I wanted to say you could come and visit us during the holidays. I didn't know you were going to be so rude and horrible. Now I think you should just buzz off," she said.

"It wasn't that we wanted to hide anything from you, dear. There was nothing planned about it. It's just the rush. We're off tomorrow," Mrs Page said. The redness had faded from her face.

She looked sad as she got to her feet. "I'm going to overlook what you said. I've known you since the day you were born. I knew your mother well. Poor Jane sometimes got funny ideas too."

I felt the room begin to sway and thought that I was going to faint. I concentrated on breathing, on keeping myself upright.

"Oh my, I'd better add the prawns before the curry sauce cooks away to nothing."

Mrs Page rushed over, took the packet out of the freezer compartment, unplugged the refrigerator and left the doors open. Beth used a clean tea towel to wipe the cutlery she'd picked up from the floor before starting to set the table. They were putting on an act, pretending that I wasn't there.

I knew that I should walk out but I couldn't. I was frozen to the spot. I watched Beth set three places, and put out glasses and ask her mother if she wanted water or a glass of wine. I had to stay, unmoving because I found that someone had balanced an apple on top of my head. If I moved I'd die.

"Will I slice the lemon, Mama," Beth asked in a little girly voice as Mr Page stepped into the kitchen carrying a bow and arrow. He ignored them the way they were ignoring me. Then he winked and took aim.

Behind him I saw Mrs Quill, her face as sharp as a ferret's, come in carrying two handbags.

"Well, what's wrong with you! Seen a ghost?" she asked me.

Slowly, I managed to lumber past her, my breath rising and falling in great gasps, keeping my head high and steady so that the apple wouldn't fall off. I knew that the arrow was aimed at the back of my skull but even so I kept going, step by step towards the front door.

WILLIAM TELL

Someone who was genuinely interested in buying Riverview turned up eventually. Before that there were a number of viewers whose chief aim was to satisfy their curiosity about my life and also some newly rich people who were part of a bubble development that would crash in a few years time.

My buyer arrived on his own. He got out of his car and stomped silently across to the tennis court. "Grand place for kids," he said.

"That's what I thought too," I agreed.

"All flown the nest? – Well, it happens."

"And I need the money. I want a quick sale," I said, in no humour for small talk.

He looked disgusted by my poor bargaining strategy. "It isn't for living-in I'd buy it," he said. "It's for development. These big houses have had their day. People want places that are small and cheap to heat. It's either that or go live in Spain."

Anyone with two pennies to rub together seemed to be headed for Spain. Winnie Page and Beth, for instance – funded by myself and all the other suckers if you thought about it. The way things were going *I'd* probably end up in a hostel for the homeless.

My fear that this was another client who would slip through

my fingers made me pull myself together and begin to point out the advantages of the location and the prime situation of the house itself. I'd had too many alecky-doos wasting my time, coming out and pulling the place apart, lifting up floor boards, bringing along architects and surveyors to look for dry rot or rising damp and then, after acting the bloody maggot, vanishing without making any sort of offer.

"I need the money because I'm moving away," I said. It was the nearest thing to a plan I'd come up with since Nat's death. As soon as I said it I saw that I would indeed leave Limerick.

"You're not a local man so," said the client.

I didn't know what I was anymore. As we stood facing each other across the wooden seat beside the court Theo came out of the house carrying a shopping bag and headed down the drive after sending us a heavy-lidded stare.

"How does the missus feel about leaving all this behind?" The man's gesture embraced the big square house, the shadow of the palm tree lying on the gravel path like a fallen sword, the daisy-spangled lawn, the tangled copse of ancient trees.

"I'm afraid she's dead," I said, stung into the admission by Theo being mistaken for my wife.

"Oh. Been here long?" he asked.

"Yes," I said.

"I'll take a look around on my own if that's alright with you," he said.

"Go ahead." I went over and sat on the painted seat beside the tennis court.

The court had not been there when we moved in. I'd had it installed during that first summer, hoping to please Jane. Tennis had been a big feature of her girlhood days in the rectory. She'd told me stories of sporty contests in which she'd carried off prizes. "It was the only thing I could ever beat Theo at." Her own mother's prowess. Midland car-journeys to clubs where everyone huddled in wooden huts between matches. Men with names like Gordon or Stuart. Someone called Cecil who'd taken her to her first dress- dance.

I'd been stupid enough to feel jealous.

112

"How come you never married one of them?"

She shook her head vehemently. "They were all creeps."

I waited, poised at the top of the drive, my senses sharpened by the thrill of possession, and the wonder of the house I'd just bought. Remember this moment, I'd told myself. We'd parked the car down on the road to add to the mystery. Jane had stopped to light a cigarette before walking up the drive. I quenched my irritation. She'd been smoking non-stop since Francesca's birth. It was bad for her. It was probably the reason why she felt so tired. But this evening I was showing her our very own Shangri-la. There was going to be no scolding, no pleading with her to take better care of herself. It was going to be love-dovey all the way.

"Sweetheart – how do you like our new home?" (I'd thought of telling her before I signed the papers, but Nat Page talked me out of it. "That's not the way to do it at all, pal. Take the bull by the horns. Present her with a fait accompli. Sure you can't pass it up, it's a steal.") He was wrong there and about other things too.

It took me some time to register that Jane's reaction was not of pleasure, but dismay. You don't expect your wife to start weeping when you give her the perfect house. "What's wrong Jane – what have I done?"

She shook her head without answering.

"You don't have to cry about it," I said.

She'd moved away from me, to crouch on the rim of the fountain. Her sobs wrenched the evening air. I felt helpless and, in a way I felt I was watching her putting on an act.

"I thought you'd be thrilled," I blurted anxiously, "what's the matter – what more do you want?"

She kept on crying. After a while she said, "I want things to be the way they were."

I reminded her of all the disadvantages of our terraced home. The awkward front steps, the cold in winter, the long narrow landing, our bedroom, cold as a country dance hall.

"Look," she said, "I'd like you to have told me beforehand. I need time to get used to the idea." Her voice was shaky but she managed the ghost of a smile.

I felt a glimmer of relief. There was nothing seriously wrong with her. Francesca was a healthy baby. The other children were getting easier to manage. Once we'd installed ourselves in here we'd be flying it. I showed her the front door key then led the way to the porch.

Moving in was hectic, but I managed it. We gave a Sunday lunchtime cocktail party shortly afterwards. It was identical to the affairs that everybody held in those days. Mushroom vol-au-vents, cocktail sausages, a hired barman, gin and tonic mixed in a jug beforehand. As many people crowded in as the house could hold. In our case we managed 80.

Jane was too thin in a red chiffon dress. Black eyeliner gave her gaze a harsh bitter cast. Her smile seemed stitched to her face. But when I went up and whispered to her asking if she was alright she nodded. "Don't worry about me, Henry," she said.

She called out to some late arrivals and hurried over to them waving her cigarette like a conductor's baton.

I breathed freely for the first time in days. The man who was going to put in the tennis court was one of the guests. When the party was over he and I paced the area where it would go. Three weeks later it was ready, net installed, white lines marked on the black tarmacadam. I felt as proud of it as I did of the house.

"Thank you, Henry," she said.

"You'll have to teach me how to play," I said melting with tenderness.

"We need tennis rackets."

"I'll buy them tomorrow," I promised.

A month later she was dead. I drove to the hospital behind the ambulance. There they asked me questions I couldn't answer.

"Date of birth?"

I could never remember birthdays. "29th of September," I said, pulling my own out of a hat.

"Ages of children?"

114

There again I was vague – except for Fran. 26th November, 1970, at Limerick Maternity Hospital.

"So the infant is only six months old," they said. They seemed unsurprised. After that they were kind enough, talking about accidents and people making mistakes.

"Was your wife complaining of feeling tired?" they asked.

"I didn't notice," I said. "We'd recently moved house. Life has been a bit hectic."

"Had she been attending a doctor?"

A guard stood in attendance, writing words in a notebook. When he was finished I signed my name and it seemed to belong to somebody else. I felt as if I'd barely survived some huge disaster such as an earthquake or a hurricane.

An older man came in, peered at me and said, "Where have I seen you before?"

I remembered exactly where and when, but pretended I didn't understand. Once Jane and I had sex in the back of my car at the side of the road between Croom and Limerick city on a warm spring night. It was during our early married years. We'd been at a housewarming in an architect's house out beside a lake. Coming home we were seized with a sudden shared mood of passion and desire that made me pull up the car in a layby. We scrambled into the back seat like a pair of kids heading for their first big sex scene. Then we were all kisses and flailing limbs, laughter and squeals and moans. We were both at boiling point when torchlight wavered at the window and the door was yanked open by a pinch-faced local sergeant who accused us of committing a public nuisance and was not swayed by the fact that we were legally married. Nat Page going to see him on my behalf was the only thing that saved us from a criminal charge.

"The poor eejit thinks sex is a sin. He'd given it up for Lent himself. He does that every year. You probably drove the hoor mad with jealousy."

The prospective buyer crunched his way back along the gravel path to where I was waiting to see him off. He definitely planned to knock the place down. Well, I didn't care. I was done with it. He'd been checking the rear premises – outhouse, utility room, a stretch of unused rooms full of junk that ran up from the study.

"I'd say you've a lot of memories," he said.

I certainly had.

On Jane's last night on earth she came home so late from shopping that I was anxious.

"I bought myself a suit," she said after she'd dumped all the grocery bags on the kitchen floor. She showed me the smart black. A Mafia widow's outfit.

"Would you not have picked something brighter," I asked.

"Get off my back," she yelled as if something had exploded in her brain.

I feared these sudden fits, like an outpouring of genuine dislike, that came over her.

"I'll go right back to the shop with it tomorrow," she spat.

I tried to ease things by beginning to empty the grocery bags: baby formula, orange juice, sausages, apples, cheese, sliced pans, soap powder.

"Give me those," She grabbed the bag of apples and the bottom of the plastic carton broke sending them scattering in all directions. Then Josh and Lynda came flying in, both of them shouting. They'd made bows and arrows from thin branches they'd found in the woods. They wanted to find a target.

"Here you are." Their mother's voice was dangerously sharp. She picked up one of the apples and placed it on her head. "Give your bow to Daddy, Josh," she said.

Josh looked discomfited. He handed the crude weapon to me with bad grace.

I can still see her: pale face, wisps flying loose from her tied back hair, her eyelashes fluttering like moths, the trembling of her lower lip, the way she stood as still as a statue.

If I'd known what she was going to do in the early hours of the following morning I'd have gone along with her William Tell routine and frightened her, not killed her. Instead I feigned amusement, getting the children to laugh with me while Jane glared and dared me to take aim.

LINKING RINGS

"Francesca, did you remember to coat the raisins with flour?"

"Yes," I lied.

"Liar." Auntie Theo snatched the wooden spoon from the draining board and began to belabour me about the head. The fruitcake she'd ordered me to make lay upturned on the cooling rack. The bottom was thickly studded with charred fruit.

I dodged out of her way yelling to be left alone. When she kept on I punched her in the chest. She stopped and we faced each other both of us breathing heavily like boxers in the ring.

"You're a bad girl, a bad, bad girl," Auntie Theo said as soon as she had enough breath.

I picked up the cake knife. If she hit me again I was going to let her have it. She was always after me. Her latest plan was to make me use up everything that was lying around in the cupboards – packets of spices and fruit, sauces, tins of cocoa, cans of pineapple.

"Children are starving," she'd say pulling open a door and taking down more stuff – sardines, packets of rice, beans with mildewed labels. She was on an economy drive. It was something that happened from time to time during which the household had to survive on its own juices so to speak. I figured she was doing it this time in an effort to stop Daddy from selling the house, but she was way too late. At that moment he was in one of the front rooms with an antique dealer trying to sell him the best of the furniture.

Now that Beth had deserted me I had to spend most of my time around the place. I'd never managed to make any other real friends. I couldn't bring them home. Auntie Theo was too weird. This cooking binge was an example. And then there was her Bible-study group. I hated the thought of someone jeering at the antics at her Bible meetings. Besides, there was no point making a new friend now. When Riverview was sold there wouldn't be a place for me to bring anyone to. I walked home from school by myself, refusing to turn my head when someone called my name. In Beth's house the blinds were all pulled down and there was no trace of human habitation.

If I could only get enough money together I'd run off to England and find Lynda. She was my one faint hope. Everyday I felt a bit more desperate.

"God will punish you, Francesca," Auntie Theo said when I came to my senses and dropped the knife. She got a foxy look in her eyes as if she was hearing some secret message. Then she waddled off and I heard her footsteps overhead in her bedroom.

I was left with only the busy cheeping of sparrows on the windowsill to disturb the peace. I sliced off a piece of cake, went over and crumbled it between my fingers, letting it cascade through the top sash onto the sill. The birds took off with a whirr of tiny wings. As I turned away I saw the furniture dealer walking past with something bulky, like cardboard, crumpled up in his grasp.

Daddy was holding a wad of bank notes. I couldn't see how much he had because when I came in he folded them and tucked them away.

"Well, that's that taken care of," he said.

I looked around, but there was nothing missing. The big oak sideboard stood in the alcove, the piano was against the wall, the pedestal table in its usual place.

"He has to come back with a van and a ladder and boxes big enough to hold the drawing room chandelier, everything is more or less fixed up. He'll take the dining-room suite as well," Daddy said.

"Did he take anything with him?" I asked, expecting Daddy to say "No".

"Only the picture."

"What picture?"

"Well not the picture, the frame. It was the right size for what he wanted. Very rare nowadays."

"What picture?" My tummy was sinking as surely as the raisins in the cake.

"That big yoke on the landing."

I stared at my father, another piece of the puzzle slipping into place. The special picture of the Madonna. That was my picture. Well, it was Mummy's picture. He had no business selling it.

"That was Mummy's," I said, the words hurting my throat.

"Actually, I bought it, Fran. Your mother didn't like it at all," he said.

I couldn't believe it! He was telling lies. That picture was my dream mother. I dashed out of the room and ran upstairs. There was this huge gap where the Madonna, my mother, had gazed at me so tenderly since I was a tiny tot. It was so much part of my life that I never found it necessary to mention it. It was as much part of me as my chin or my little toe. You don't go around talking about things that are so obviously there.

Without it the landing felt huge and unfriendly. It was like the rest of the world, stretching out around me full of unhappiness and danger. I needed my special picture. Nobody should touch it without my permission. I had once mentioned at the tea table that I'd seen the lady move, but I got such a teasing that I promised I was only making it up. Later I'd gone up to tell her I was sorry and she'd leaned out and stroked my cheek with her silken hand and there was the scent of roses. For a short time I hoped that I was becoming a saint like Saint Therese of Lisieux, the Little Flower.

I returned to Daddy in the front room. He was pulling a bottle of whiskey out of the sideboard cupboard.

"You've got to get the picture back," I said. "I'll pay you for it." I had about £50.00 in the Post Office.

He puckered up his face and looked into the whiskey glass.

"Can't be done," he said.

The sun was streaking through the window and the liquid in his glass made rings of light dance on the sideboard's surface.

"I want that picture."

"Better to let it go," he said. "We'd have nowhere big enough to hang it. I bought that picture for a song in an auction in a parish priest's house, your Mummy nearly threw me out when I brought it home."

"I need it," I said. Just thinking about it being taken away made me feel how huge the world was and how lonely.

"We'll get you another one. Something less like a chocolate box. Okay kiddo?" He wasn't even listening. "He's a decent skin. He gave a fair price. He's taking the pedestal table as well, and the oak one from the hall. And, of course, the chandelier and a few other things."

"I don't care about anything else. Get my picture back!" I wailed.

It was like talking to a deaf person.

Daddy shook his head. "What's the point? It wasn't valuable. It was only a print. As a matter of fact, he didn't even take it. He cut it out and stuck it in the dustbin. He only wanted the frame."

I remembered the man passing the window as I threw out cake crumbs. I gasped, realising what had happened. Then I charged out to the yard and lifted the bin lid. A corner of a large canvas stuck up out of the mounds of vegetable peelings and plastic bags. I wiped at the surface and recognised the familiar creamy folds of her gown, the edge of her blue shawl. It was beyond rescue because it had been broken into several pieces. It was as bad as finding that someone you loved had been chopped to pieces. I ran upstairs to my room, shaking. No wonder my mother had killed herself.

I began to see links and connections I'd never noticed before. They wanted Auntie Theo out of the way, and they wanted me out of the way with her. It had nothing to do with money. Daddy wasn't that hard up. He owned an office. He had a lady-friend in Dublin. He'd probably had one all the time, even when my mother was alive. Mr Page hadn't taken his money. He and Daddy had always been friends. It was a trick so that he could sell the house.

I shuddered with apprehension. I'd thought I had a family, but they were disappearing before my eyes. Soon I'd have nobody to turn to. I faced the terrifying prospect of Auntie Theo and myself. It was possible that she was part of the plot. "Leave Francesca to me," I could hear her voice. If she got me trapped on my own I'd be her slave. I'd have to join her horrible prayer group. I'd be sent out to knock on doors asking people to repent of their sins. I could feel her hand smiting my cheek for some miniscule offence, the crack of a wooden spoon because I'd left a speck of dust on a piece of furniture or lint on the carpet. And it was all Daddy's fault. He was the juggler twirling the rings, spinning them out and holding them up for examination to show that they could not be separated and then, with one quick flick of the wrist throwing them to the four winds.

"Well, children, the deal is done. Riverview is sold." He had the nerve to attempt a smile as he came in to break the news at the supper table. "I've just had a call from the buyer. Everything is taken care of."

"So – what happens now?" Josh asked.

I watched closely, hoping to find some crack that would reveal what they were up to.

Auntie Theo had reappeared with her pouchy cheeks heavily

rouged. She'd cooked rice and mixed it with tinned fish and frozen peas. Alice was eating hers as if it was the best thing she'd ever tasted. Josh was sitting at the end of the table, his plate on top of a newspaper, doing a crossword at the same time as he ate.

"Well bugger that," he said, crossing out a word he'd just filled in.

"Did you hear what I said?" Daddy asked and they all, except Auntie Theo, nodded.

If I lived with Auntie Theo I'd never be able to go to a disco, or the cinema. We probably wouldn't even have television because she thought it was a bad influence. There'd be nothing but Bible-study groups, bazaars and sessions with old Sibyl looking into my mug of tea and waffling on about destiny and fools. I'd be better off in an enclosed order of nuns. I'd be better off running away.

"Oh please!" I looked around the table at everyone minding their own business. I wanted us all to link hands, or say we'd stay together or something but I didn't have the right words.

LINKING RINGS

Selling Riverview was a great weight off my mind. Maybe the fact that the buyer intended to raze the place to the ground and make a lot of money by building apartment blocks was not quite right. The house had an interesting history. It had been the birthplace of a well-known politician. One of its earliest occupants was an eminent landscape painter. It was rumoured that a nineteenth-century republican uprising had been plotted in the drawing-room. There were associations with a lady writer and a gentleman horticulturist. The first owner had been a personal friend of Daniel O'Connell. The great man had spent a night in the west bedroom, Josh's room. I could easily imagine the heritage people protesting, staging sit-downs in front of the gates to stop the demolition gang from moving in. That was their problem. They didn't need the money the way I did. I was careful not to divulge details of the sale to anyone.

In a way, I didn't even feel that the house had ever belonged to me. Jane's death so soon after we'd moved in robbed me of the delights of being a man of property. All it ever was without her was a place to leave the children while I went about rebuilding some sort of life for myself. I felt no pangs whatsoever about selling it to someone who was going to raze it to the ground. I just concentrated on getting the deal done. Theo, of course, was a problem. I badly wanted to visit Myrna but every time I made plans to go to see her something prevented me.

Unfortunately, the Dublin office had been closed down. Matters in Limerick remained undecided. My bank manager grew more morose and unhappy at every encounter. The news that I had found a buyer brought merely the sourest smile to his face. Only the auctioneer remained full of bonhomie and reassurances that my prayers had been answered. He kept telling me how lucky I'd been to shift my outsize residence.

I recalled the fantasies I'd indulged in back in the balmy days when Nat came to me to tell me to buy it. "You'll be King of the Castle, boy," he'd enthused. I'd felt excited. I'd made it! Life was perfect.

On the day he came to me to tell me it was available I came home bursting with the news and found Jane sitting listlessly in the front room with a wailing Francesca. Down in the big bare playroom the children were romping around unchecked. Our current home help was nowhere in sight. When I spoke to Jane she said that her head hurt. I kissed her forehead, the news of Riverview on the tip of my tongue. Before I could speak she got to her feet and lumbered from the room. I felt hurt but comforted myself with the fun I would have when I surprised her with the news of my big purchase.

"So, what's going to happen now?" Josh asked, then shovelled a forkful of white mush into his mouth.

"You were thinking of buying one of those nice little town houses," Alice said. She looked brightly at Theo who grunted as she lowered herself onto a stool.

Was I? I didn't think so. My plan at the moment was to find someplace cheap to rent.

Josh drummed some jungle beat on the tabletop. I wondered how he could eat, do a crossword and keep a tune in his head while holding a conversation.

"There wouldn't be room for us in one of those town houses, there's hardly room to swing a cat," I said.

"You don't have to worry about us, Dad, we told you that," Alice said.

"Suppose Lynda comes home?" I suggested.

"She won't." Alice was certain.

My chief worry, of course, was how to get rid of Theo. I must break any links there were between us. We weren't even blood relations. She had no hold on me. Getting rid of her was not going to be pleasant.

During the following days I was a coward, keeping out of her way, hoping she would come up with some solution of her own accord. I wondered if she had any relatives who would take her in. My family's fury over my marriage to Jane came back to haunt me: "You know who she comes from?", "Bad stock", "It's them that sent half the country off to America in coffin ships", "Not a stick or stone left of your Grandaddy's house".

When Jane killed herself not one of my own came near me. I knew they'd have seen it as proof that they'd been right about her all along. If they'd helped a little I wouldn't have ended up with my present problems.

Now both my parents were long dead. My one remaining aunt was in a nursing home. I hadn't heard from my brother in Australia since he emigrated. As for my sisters? I'd forgotten them as completely as they'd forgotten me. I was like the uncle who, in a previous generation, emigrated to San Francisco and never made contact again.

I thought of Nat Page. How would he have acted? Easy. He wouldn't have let Theo in the door in the first place. "Henry, I'm, warning you, the only way you'll get rid of that one is by shooting her," he'd said. "Sure she thinks she owns the place," he complained when we arrived back late one evening to find her and her friends singing hymns around the piano in the front room. "Are you sure your children are safe with those crazy people?" he'd asked.

"At least she doesn't bring strange men into the house," I said.

"The couple of specimens I saw singing looked as nutty as fruitcakes," he said. "But I get the drift. There's no sex – we hope!" He snorted in derision.

But Nat was gone with last year's snow and my hard-earned money. As I worked at tying up loose ends I asked myself again why I'd kept Riverview on for all the intervening years after Jane's suicide and could come up with no sensible reason. Apathy? Pride? I recollected a feeling of wanting to show the world, of not giving in, of being as good as the next one – maybe proving my own blamelessness by refusing to be ousted from my mansion. Perhaps I'd turned into a replica of the villainous Smyth-Drummond. Maybe that was what Jane had seen in me and why she'd killed herself. The big shot with the big house who had no idea of the suffering going on under his nose. I shivered at the suspicion that she had hated me when she died.

In early June I sat in a solicitor's office finalising the sale. It was a straightforward arrangement. The buyer had made his money in the building business in England. Ready cash was being paid into my bank. I'd be able to settle my debts and hang onto what was left of my business. I felt as if I'd been thrown a lifebelt. I could last out until the tide turned.

Later, walking along the busy pavements of the city, I felt myself bobbing along in the crowd. My arms were tired as if I'd been performing a juggling act, linking and unlinking rings ad nauseum. My head began to spin. The rings turned into individuals. Myrna, Fran, Nat Page, Theo, the house buyer, Lynda . . . Lynda! I'd almost forgotten about my vanished daughter. Out of sight out of mind! Was that the sort of person I was?

I came to a halt. Someone asked if I felt unwell. I pushed them away and staggered into the lounge bar of the Royal George Hotel where I recovered over a double Scotch with ice.

"I'm Henry Cleeve, civil engineer," I told myself. "Prominent business man. The man who was responsible for almost every feckin' water scheme in the city."

126

"I had a long and successful career. He will be sadly missed," I told myself. That was the sort of rubbish journalists wrote when people like Nat died.

I decided to take a taxi back to Riverview. On the journey out I rehearsed how I was going to put the case to Theo. She must make her own arrangements. She could go back to where she came from. It had been very good of her and all that – no, better not mention any favours done. My arguments went round in circles, breaking up and regrouping – Jane, her own life, the end of the road, regrettable but necessary, Jane, the house.

When I got to Riverview I was met by an unforeseen hitch. There'd been a row. I couldn't speak to Theo because she'd barricaded herself in her room. Fran, very subdued, broke the news. I climbed up the stairs and banged on her door. No sound came from the other side. I tried the handle and found it locked.

"Theo, we need to talk," I said, my face close to the painted wood. Then I waited feeling foolish and getting no response. She'd have to come out sometime. She'd have to eat – and drink.

"You can get typhoid fever from drinking water from washbasins," I told the door.

It was like talking to nothing. My head was beginning to spin again. All my troubles and vicissitudes whirled around me like rings around a planet. My knees felt as if they were about to buckle.

I went up to my own room and threw myself on the bed and thought how simple it would be to lie down and die. The wavy lines and bumps on the ceiling shifted under my gaze like pictures in a fire throwing out images. A woman's nose, a wrinkled hand, insect shapes. Then, as I drifted into sleep, everything broke apart and became wheeling fireworks.

When I woke up it was dark. I lay there picking out the shapes of the heavy pieces of furniture. There was a lot more clearing out to be done. I turned my gaze towards the window and watched the dark outlines of trees still as sentinels in the windless night.

CUP AND BALL

The reason Auntie Theo locked herself in her room was because she claimed I'd brandished the sweeping brush at her. It wasn't true. I'd been trying to reach a cobweb and she came up behind me and I let the brush fall. She'd been holed up in her room for nearly a week. Of course, I'd heard her creeping to the bathroom in the middle of the night when she was sure Daddy was gone to bed. And in the morning the kitchen sink had a dish with Weetabix crumbs in it so I knew that she wasn't starving. And, of course, when we were out of the house at work or in school she had the run of the place. It was like living with a very cunning rat. I didn't mind because it kept her off my back.

Josh said the row wasn't my fault. Auntie Theo wanted to declare war on Daddy because he was going to give her her walking papers. I didn't know whether he was serious or not. The two of us were in the morning room and he was showing me a musical trick and I was happy to have him paying attention to me. Every so often he was really nice and acted like a proper brother.

"Look Fran," he held up a two-pronged fork. "This is for tuning."

We didn't call it the morning room, we called it the front room. "Morning room" was the name given on the old bell board which was still fixed on the wall in the downstairs bathroom. It was there because the downstairs bathroom used to be a butler's pantry. The bell board was defunct because Daddy had disconnected it years ago.

Josh fiddled around. I wasn't really interested in learning about tuning forks. I was born with a tin ear. (Not even Auntie Theo was able to make me join in and sing hymns with her while she played the piano practising for a prayer meeting.)

"It's a pity these don't work," I said pushing the defunct ivory button set in the round mahogany plaque beside the fireplace.

"Lynda and I had great sport ringing them," Josh said, tapping the tuning fork against the black marble of the fireplace. "Then Mummy got furious." He looked sadly at the useless knob. Then, he took a ping-pong ball, a piece of string and a plastic cup out of his gear bag.

"Fill that cup right up with water, Fran, and I'll show you something," Josh said.

I had nothing else to do so I went out to the kitchen and turned on the cold tap. I remembered what Daddy had said about catching typhoid if you drank bedroom tap water and I hoped that Auntie Theo did and caught the disease. As I filled the cup at the kitchen sink I heard an enormous thump overhead in her room. Just one. Then silence. I waited but nothing more happened. Maybe she was trying to knock the house down. The idea made me giggle. She was going to have to come out sometime. I thought of all the times she'd locked me up. Now she'd done it to herself. If I was Daddy I'd board up the door and window of her room and leave her there for the next owner to find, like a nun walled up in a convent because she'd broken some rule.

"I'm not going to sing," I said to Josh as I walked back into the room.

"You can say that again. I wouldn't inflict it on myself. This has nothing to do with singing," Josh said. He squeezed a dab of superglue onto the end of the twine and pressed it against the ping-pong ball. That's another thing – he's very clever with his hands. In a few seconds he was dangling the little celluloid ball in front of me and asking me to hold the string.

I obeyed.

I was hoping to talk to Josh about my future and I could only do so by pretending to be interested in his tricks. I was getting worried because everything about my future seemed so vague. Josh knew what he was going to do. He'd already bought his ticket for London. But I needed advice, or, at least, someone to tell me that they cared about what happened to me. Alice was too gooey about Mark to be bothered and Lynda was gone. Josh was my only hope.

"There – you see!" he sounded pleased as the little white globe started jumping around in all directions.

"Keep your hand still," he said.

"I am keeping it still," I said. This was boring, boring. If I had to do it for much longer I'd start to yawn.

"Would you like to play chess?" I suggested.

I'm pretty good. Daddy taught me one wet Christmas. The thing about a chess game is that it goes on for a long time and you can ask your opponent all sorts of questions – like "Will you help me to get some money so that I can run away?" Or, "Won't you tell me where you're staying in London?"

Josh was too busy scowling at the ball to even answer my suggestion about chess. Next he tipped it very, very gently with the tuning fork and watched as it looped the loop and spun and twirled.

"Know what that proves?" he asked.

It proved that one of us was insane.

"I wish that I was at least 23 years old," I said.

"Know what I wish," Josh said, "I wish I had a job in television. Local radio sucks. They're paying me peanuts. The first thing I'll do when I get to London is go round the studios. If I don't get anything there I'll move on to Germany."

"That's not fair!" I wailed.

"Why isn't it?"

"Everyone except me is going someplace."

"Yes. Well, you're only a kid. But when you get to my age there's nothing here. Everything is pretty well washed up," Josh said. "Now answer my question – tell me what that proves." (Amazingly, during this exchange the ping-pong ball continued bouncing on the end of the string.)

"I don't know what it proves. I don't want to be left with Auntie Theo."

"It proves that sound is a form of energy," Josh said.

"You're hitting it with that thing. That's why it's moving." I had no idea why we were having this mindless conversation when there were all sorts of urgent things to say.

Josh made a mock bow. "Now my little assistant," he said, "I am about to give another demonstration to prove that it is the natural vibration of the tuning fork that causes the ping-pong ball to move."

The trouble with Josh was that you never could have a normal conversation with him. When Beth was my friend we made fun of him, but now, without her, I had nobody to talk to about how odd he was even if he was kind underneath.

"Beth and Mrs Page are going to live in Spain," I said, hoping he'd be interested.

"They've already gone," he said.

Holding the twine was beginning to make me feel sick because of the ball of stuff lodged in my stomach which still hurt.

"Here," he said, taking the string from my grasp and giving me the plastic cup I'd filled with water in the kitchen. "Now I'm going to show you something even more exciting."

That wouldn't be hard. Two snails climbing up a wall would do it.

"It's all about sound," Josh said, "Sound and power." He stood so close to me that I could smell his socks and dipped the tuning fork into the water in the cup. Nothing happened except that I remembered the big bang I'd heard coming from Auntie Theo's room while I was in the kitchen.

"Sound is vibration, Fran, remember that," Josh said. "It is what makes things move. It is the big mover."

He peered at me, hoping that I was impressed.

I remembered a rude fact a girl in school had told us about vibrating. She showed us a long yoke with a battery that she'd found in her mother's dressing table drawer. Beth and I hadn't believed a word of it.

Josh hit the tuning fork against the mantelpiece and held it out to me before dipping it into the water.

"See what I mean?" he laughed as the water splashed up into my face and down my front.

I yelped and jumped back.

"Sound and power, Fran," he said.

"A funny noise came from Auntie Theo's room," I said, remembering. "A really big bang, like something fell – a body or something like that."

"You heard her fall and you never went to look!"

"I didn't say that she'd fallen. I said something crashed."

"Is she alright?"

"How would I know?" I said. "I was getting the water for you, remember."

"But something happened to her."

"I only heard a noise," I said, "It just sounded loud."

Josh raced upstairs ahead of me. The door was still locked. When we hammered on the centre panel we heard nothing. I felt that she was sitting on her bedside chair waiting like a spider to catch flies, but Josh disagreed. He gathered himself together, then charged at the door like a bull at a gate. There was a splintering sound, a roar from him and the door flew open as the lock burst. He staggered in rubbing his shoulder.

Auntie Theo lay on the carpet in a muddle of clothes and hangers, pinned down by the wardrobe that had fallen on top of her. She was dead. I was sure for a moment that she was dead. How could I explain my feeling of joy that I turned into a fit of coughing? Hallelujahs rang in my head. I was as wicked as she said I was and I didn't care.

And then as Josh grunted and tugged and lifted the piece of furniture a little she groaned and it was evident that she was still alive. I wished he wasn't with me. I wished I'd come up and broken in by myself and lifted the wardrobe again and again letting it fall back on her head until she was done for.

CUP AND BALL

As the car reached the end of the speed-limit zone on the outskirts of Castletroy I pressed down on the accelerator and my heart lifted. I thought of the G-string in the glove compartment. It had lain there since the trip to Connemara. I had come on it by chance as I looked for a biro pen. As I weighed the flimsy nonsense in my hand the thought of Myrna worked its magic. I needed her. I felt the roundness of her fleshy buttocks warm under the palms of my hands. Her laughter sounded in my ears. My lips softened as my mouth opened to receive her first kiss. "Belated Happy Birthday," I'd say. "Help me, Myrna. I love you my witch of the wood. I want to eat you. I want to do this, and this. We must never be away from each other for this long again."

I had come from the hospital where the doctor drew a diagram on a scrap of paper and talked about balls, sockets, grooves and flexibility and explained Theo's injuries.

"She's quite elderly," he said. "Her bones have become brittle. The first thing she needs is a hip replacement." He indicated his sketch.

"It sounds like an engineering job," I said.

"It is an engineering job," he answered.

We were standing by a window in the hospital corridor. Theo

lay, semi-conscious, in a room close by with its door open. She was snoring lightly. She'd been taken to the operating theatre where some preliminary work was done on her hip.

I thought of the wardrobe she had pulled down on top of herself through some unfortunate manoeuvre. I was more annoyed at this addition to my troubles, which seemed to be proliferating like a plague of locusts, than sorry for her.

"Will she be alright?" I asked to hide my lack of concern. "Of course we can't guarantee that she'll be dancing the cancan," the doctor said. "But she'll be hobbling around in no time. The pin we plan to insert will see to that."

He tucked the scraps of paper back into the pocket of his white coat and strode away down the corridor. It was a bright sunny day.

Outside I walked to my car, got in, opened the glove compartment in an absentminded way, found the G-string, and was at once seized by a lustfulness that reminded me that I wanted love and sex as much as the next man and there hadn't much of it around lately.

I refused to allow Theo's calamity to weigh on my mind. I'd arrived home two afternoons ago to find Josh and Fran struggling to rescue her. It seemed that she'd been standing on a chair and toppled off. What she'd been doing standing on a chair in front of her wardrobe was a mystery. One thing was clear, she'd had a narrow escape and was bloody lucky to be alive.

Josh, showing more good sense that I'd have given him credit for, had already called for an ambulance when I arrived.

"It's a good thing for your woman that she didn't crack her skull open," I said to the nurse who appeared at my elbow asking me to sign a form naming myself as Theo's next of kin shortly after we arrived in the hospital.

"I'm not exactly kin," I said. "She's just a family connection."

"The patient is lucky her injuries aren't more serious," the girl said sniffily. "However, I'd better warn you she's very confused. Somebody has to be responsible for her. I take it that she lives in your house."

"I don't have a house. It's been sold."

"I believe that it was in your residence that the accident occurred." The nurse's voice dropped below freezing. "You are the householder, are you not?"

I had a horrible presentiment that this could end up with Theo suing me. Reluctantly, I took the form and signed my name.

I stopped off on my way to Dublin and telephoned the house. Fran answered. She sounded breathless as if she'd been running. I told her not to expect me until the day after tomorrow. A few things in Dublin needed my immediate attention.

"Daddy – can I come?" she asked in a tiny voice.

I thought of Myrna's place and how impossible it would be. "Not this time," I said. "Ask a friend round. I'll be back tomorrow or the day after."

"A letter came from Lynda," Fran said. Her voice was barely audible. "She's in Croydon. She sent an address."

"Good," I said. "That's great news. You can tell me all about it when I get home."

"She's having a baby," Fran said.

I had no idea of how a parent in these times dealt with such matters. We'd had the Kerry babies tragedy and the young girl in Granard found dead with her newborn infant at the foot of a statue of the virgin. Thank God Lynda was an adult. I supposed she was able to take care of herself. I hoped she was alright. I felt totally inadequate.

"Are you there, Daddy?" Fran's voice floated up out of the black cup of the receiver.

"I'm here. I'm listening," I said. Static crackled on the wire.

"Josh will see her when he goes over. She sounds really happy," Fran said. Then, her words bouncing out like balls thrown at a target, she announced, "I want to go with him. He says I can if you give me the money."

She was trying it on. It was out of the question. I refused to have this sort of discussion at long distance.

"Take it easy," I said. "We can't talk about something so important now. I'll be home tomorrow or the day after. We'll have a chat then. You're way too young for London."

The receiver at the other end clattered back into its cradle. I dialled the first few numbers to make a reconnection, then changed my mind, fuelled by my desire to make haste to Dublin.

It had never occurred to me that Myrna would not be there. The thought of her getting up from her chair tucked in the nook beside the bar to welcome me had been in my head all the way up. She was wearing my favourite green dress. It emphasised the soft bloom of her throat.

But, sadly, there was no Myrna. I stood, perplexed and discomfited looking at the strange woman behind the reception desk who said that Miss Brophy was not around.

"Miss Brophy!" At first the name meant nothing. "Are you a regular visitor? I can't say I recall your face," she said. She had big teeth that clicked shut like a trap when she'd finished speaking.

"I stay here quite often," I said. I was in no mood to divulge any details.

"Let me see," she trawled a pudgy finger along the lines of the opened ledger. "I'm not sure that we can fit you in."

"If you check with Myrna – with Miss Brophy I'm sure she'll insist that you find me a room," I said.

"I can hardly do that," the woman said. "She's out of the country."

"And when will she be back?"

She shrugged. "Next week. The week after."

My sense of deflation increased. I became aware that I was holding the package with the G-string in the hand that was not clutching my briefcase. The woman had fixed her eyes on it and I had the uneasy feeling that she could see through the wrapping, like an X-ray machine.

"I should have phoned ahead," I said, feeling miserable.

The toothy woman sized me up then she said, with a take it or leave it attitude, "You can have number thirteen. It's on the top floor."

Number thirteen, lucky for some.

It was cramped and low-ceilinged, up at the attic level that would have been the servants' quarters in a bygone age. The furnishings were sparse, the bathroom not en suite but a Spartan affair with a cobwebby skylight and shared with another bedroom across the small landing. I didn't want to be there, but I didn't want to be anywhere else. It was a test, a trial I had to submit to and endure with good grace because of the offhand way I'd behaved towards Myrna. Even the wardrobe was low-sized and so skimpy that my suit jacket wouldn't fit into it without my twisting the hanger sideways.

I folded it and placed it over the back of a wobbly chair, put my few belongings into one of the newspaper-lined drawers in a pine chest, took my turn in the uncomfortable bathroom and decided to go out for a quick meal with the evening paper. On my way I bought myself a bottle of Jameson in an off licence. I planned to go back and make the best of a disappointing situation by getting well and truly plastered while lying in bed. I was not even going to ask where exactly Myrna had gone. She often took quick trips with a girlfriend to lie in the sun and read blockbusters. It was no business of mine how she occupied herself when I wasn't around. It was a free world.

The bistro I ate in was nearby and unremarkable. The food was basic, the place practically empty. I was placed at a window table so that I felt I was on display as passers by paused and pressed their faces against the glass to examine the quality of my grilled lamb chops and mixed vegetables. The bill when it came was exorbitant and I had a bad moment when after handing over my credit card I became convinced that my bank account was almost empty and the card would be rejected. My relief when it was honoured made me overtip and hate myself for such weak-mindedness.

When I returned to the hotel the late night drinkers were beginning to show up. It was later than I thought – 11.00. I nodded at those I recognised and was struck by an air of secrecy, of bottled-up merriment.

A man clearly in his cups came up and slapped me on the shoulder. "Can you bate it," he said. "And fair dues to her. Though I never thought I'd see the day. I'd have put my money on yourself if I was asked. Seems you were the loser in the end."

For a moment I was back in the school classroom in Ennis, Nat Page beside me playing a furtive game of pontoon under the cover of the desk top. As always he was the dealer. As always I'd lost the few shillings I owned. The teacher strode towards us and by some sleight of hand the cards had been slipped into my satchel between the chipped mug and an old sliothar, souvenir of a victory on the hurling field, in the front pocket.

"What are you having, it's all on the house," the man said, he had had a fair few drinks himself.

"Coffee," I said, thinking of the bottle of whiskey upstairs. I wondered what was being celebrated – a big win at the races? – Or maybe we had a lottery millionaire in our midst.

"You can't be drinking coffee, not on a night like this. It's not every day that our Myrna gets herself married." He leered at me in boozy triumph.

He was still grinning at me when a journalist, who wrote a political column for a national newspaper and often used opinions expressed in the small hours in the bar by unsuspecting drunks to pad out his column, nudged me from the other side.

"Hey, Henry. Our favourite girl got herself married today. She telephoned from Rome about two hours ago. Fair dues to her.

Slipped away and did it quietly. Says she didn't want a whole lot of fuss and codology. Ah well, it was good while it lasted. She had a soft spot for you."

He studied me over the tops of his horn-rimmed spectacles with his night owl stare. "You were fond of her too."

"Married – why?" I asked as I tried to grasp what he was saying.

"The same reason anyone does. A certain time in your life, a certain mood, a notion that it's probably for the best. Did you get a chance to talk to her lately?" he asked.

"No," I said. "Not for a while."

"She felt she needed to think of the future. It happens. Makes the world go round."

Shock flamed in my cheeks as I thought of the silly underwear thrown upstairs on my uncomfortable bed. I felt as foolish as an outraged rooster. I thought of the long drive back to Limerick and the fact that I was too tired to attempt it.

"This is a great little establishment. One of the last relics of oul' decency. It'll be a pity to see it go, but it will. She'll be living in Rome," the journalist said.

"Why Rome?" I asked stupidly.

"Because that's where the fella is from. He came over here for a trade show and it seems they fell for each other right away."

I felt a sort of flatness, a sense of anti-climax. She'd gone off with an Italian. I'd been feeling bad about not coming up to see her, about staying away without explanation, and I probably hadn't even crossed her mind. She had a whole life of her own. I listened to the buzz around me. Everyone was talking about her good news. I was the only one not in the know. I felt like a pariah as I furtively made my way upstairs.

In room thirteen I undressed and climbed into bed. I filled the cup I'd drunk my coffee from with a generous helping of whiskey and propped myself up with my pillows. I lay awake long after I'd finished it. Ballad singing and the heavy smell of cigarette smoke wafted up to the top floor as I made my way across to the bathroom to fill the cup from the cold water tap and rinse my parched mouth. I remembered warning Theo about the dangers of typhoid inherent in such a practice. That's how the writer, Arnold Bennett, died. There were worse ways. Hanging. I looked up at the long thin cord dangling from the dusty skylight and my eyes squirted foolish tears.

Back in my bed I tried to rationalise my feelings. What had I expected? I'd never contemplated marrying Myrna myself. But why not? Now that it was impossible I pictured the two of us with a house of babies, me parading her through a giddy social whirl of congratulations and festive occasions. And she'd have been kind and helpful with Fran. She needed a mother. I saw Myrna in a red and gold brocade dress I'd spotted recently in a boutique's window. I'd thought how the colour would suit her bright sunny curls. Then the curls became sleek black tresses and the woman in the red and gold dress changed into Jane. Whiskey slopped onto my pillow.

"Now you see me, now you don't," Jane said.

She walked behind a curtain and remerged in a twinkle wearing a strapless, bouffant black taffeta gown. We were on our way to a dance in Jury's Hotel. An elderly shopkeeper with a poncy accent moved in on her immediately. I watched him across the room, his nose stuck down the cleavage, a happy smile on his face.

"Where did you go to?" I asked Jane some hours later.

"I hid," she said sharply. "He was disgusting and you didn't care. You didn't come to my rescue. You were too busy watching the other women."

Her accusation was unfair. I'd danced with Winnie Page. I'd danced twice with a blonde German lady with a formidable bosom. I'd spent a lot of time at the bar counter with the other men. I didn't know that she wanted me to rescue her.

"Jane," I said hoarsely to the empty room and realised that I'd had far too much to drink.

As I drifted off into uneasy sleep that long ago occasion in Jury's seemed to be going on in another dimension. I recollected driving home from it. I deliberately slowed the car as we passed the gates of Riverview. I imagined her surprise, myself turning the key in the lock, then hurrying through the rooms, throwing the doors open to display its delights to Jane.

I jolted back to full consciousness, the way you do when a sudden falling sensation wrecks your drifting into sleep.

All of that – the dance, the house, Jane in her short black strapless frock were in the past, locked behind the impenetrable barriers built by time. And now Myrna was married and there was no corner in her life for me except this miserable attic bedroom. The realisation gave me one of those moments of truth that can visit you in the darkest hours of the night. Nat was part of it too, part of the past. My own individual past. Not yours.

The past was not for remembering, it was a mockery. It blocked me off from everything I treasured – my treasures on earth. As surely as the lumpy mattress dug into my spine I felt it like a black force pushing me onward to where I didn't want to go.

So what use were my memories? Of no more use than a handful of old bones. As I reached this nadir of pessimism my own bones began to shake with grief and I realised that I was far from dead and that for as long as I was alive Jane would be too.

Finally the doctor with his diagrams floated into the room. Cup and ball! What was I going to do about Theo?

EATING CIGARETTES

I can't describe how lonely I felt after Daddy went off to Dublin, leaving me behind in Riverview. The quietness in the house was as thick as smoke. It stifled all noise, making even the birdsong in the garden sound muffled. I began to feel as if I was the only person in the world. A girl Robinson Crusoe, shipwrecked on the flotsam of a house. I brought Dusty in for company, but he was no help. He flopped under the coat hooks in the back hall with his head on his paws only giving his tail an occasional twitch to show that he was alive.

I'd never been so completely on my own before. There was always someone around – Auntie Theo more than likely. I went out into the yard and lifted the lid of the dustbin. The broken corner of the Madonna canvas still poked its way out of the rubbish and made me cry hopelessly. If I had to stay here on my own for long I'd go mad. I ran back into the house, threw myself on the sofa in the drawing room and buried my face in the cushions. It was like being in a dead house. Everywhere I looked there were gaps. Objects that were part of my whole life had vanished. The marble table on which Auntie Theo set out the food for her Bible-study group was gone. So was the large painting of trees that hung over the fireplace. And there was only one sofa. The green velvet chaise longue that belonged in front of the large wall mirror was missing.

I began to believe that Daddy had abandoned me deliberately. He'd been jumpy and his face went funny when I'd asked him what time he'd be back before he went to the hospital. I might never see him again. I looked out the window at the hedges. They seemed to have shot up like the briars that encircled the Sleeping Beauty's palace. I could be here forever by myself. Daddy had said he was going to Dublin. I went over everything I knew about his life when he was away from us. I knew he had a companion. She'd never seemed like a real person before. Now I saw that she was dangerous. She wanted to steal him for herself. And, to make things worse, I didn't have an address or telephone number to contact him. I didn't even know this woman's name.

"A certain person," Auntie Theo called her. "A lady who should not be mentioned in polite circles."

Something told me that if his friend was a friendly person he'd have taken me to Dublin to meet her instead of leaving me on my own. Or else he'd have told Josh to bring me over to London for a little holiday. We surely had enough money to pay for that.

I thought about Lynda. I'd told him about Lynda's letter and that she was having a baby and he didn't even seem to think it was important. It could wait until he came home today or tomorrow. He'd just been fooling me. All he wanted was to get away without us. He wasn't a proper father at all.

After a while I lifted my head from the cushions feeling a little calmer. My tummy rumbled. I'd have to see if there was anything to eat in the fridge. Daddy had left some cash on the mantelpiece beside Josh's cup and ball vibrations stuff. There was £30.00, but I didn't want to spend it. I might need it to help me escape.

Out in the kitchen I reread Lynda's letter. It was a good letter. She even said, "Tell Auntie Theo I was asking for her." The important thing was that she was with the kissogram boy. She'd written "Tarzan!" in brackets. She loved him. She hadn't thought that she did, but now she knew she wanted to stay with him. She was having a baby. She was sorry she hadn't had a chance to say a real goodbye, except to Fran. When I got to that bit tears rolled down my cheeks and I realised that she was my very favourite person.

The baby would be born in September, so maybe by Christmas they would be able to come home for a visit. It struck me that she didn't know that the house was sold. There were lots of things she didn't know. She didn't know that Auntie Theo was in hospital. If she knew that I was here all by myself she'd have said, "Why don't you come over here. You can help me mind the baby." They'd moved into a very nice flat. She gave the address. It was in a part of London called Croydon. "It's very easy to find," she said. "Hoping to hear from you soon," she finished off. At the very end was a PS but she had drawn a line through it. I knew what she'd been going to say even though she hadn't written it down. "Fran you must come over." I could see the words appearing on the page the way they do when you write them down in invisible ink and then heat the paper. I got matches and lit one under the space but my hands were trembling and before the blue handwriting could show itself the paper caught fire and I had to drop it very quickly into the sink and turn on the cold tap.

I began to wander from room to room. All the time I thought about Lynda. Soon I became absolutely certain that she wanted me to go over to her. After all, she'd cut off a lock of hair and given it to me especially so I'd remember her. I was the person she would want to have around if she was having a baby. I was old enough to be an au pair. Beth and I sometimes babysat for the people that lived next door to the Pages.

But I wasn't going to think about Beth anymore. I hated her. She'd deceived me. Our friendship was finished forever.

I returned to the kitchen and opened cupboard doors finding tinned tomatoes, sardines, a packet of ground almonds, a pot of jam. The only thing in the freezer compartment of the fridge was a tray of ice cubes. In the fridge itself were some soggy mushrooms and a few pieces of dried up ham along with a carton of sour milk and a jar of mayonnaise. The only object left in the top cupboard in the kitchen was the lidless teapot. I took it down and found a spider had made it its home. Then I sat on a kitchen stool and pulled some threads out of my jeans to make the knee gashes bigger. After that I frayed the ends.

There were nightdresses and vests and knickers and big bodices belonging to Auntie Theo hanging on the clothes horse in front of the range although the range was not lit. I took them off it and made them into a bundle and carried them up to her room.

It was what I needed – a good excuse to go into her bedroom. She wouldn't want her underwear left out for the whole world to see.

The moment I opened the door the stuffiness hit me in the face. It was mostly from stale cigarette smoke. There were fag ends in the lids of cold-cream jars and on the mantelpiece in saucers and dropped into an empty jam jar on the floor beside the unmade bed. The wardrobe was still overturned.

The first thing I did was pull up the blankets and coverlet which smelt heavy and sour. I couldn't do anything about the wardrobe, it was too heavy. I went over to the window and tugged it open and when I did I heard men talking.

I stuck my head out and saw them below me, on the path that ran along by the side of the house between the small crescent lawn edged with raised flower beds and the border with its rosebushes and weeds. The garden was very straggly from lack of attention. The only colour was a few pinks, a tumble of nasturtiums and a veronica bush with purple flowers. All the ancient roses had withered on the stalk.

One of the men was Billy Kelly our house painter. I guessed almost immediately that the other man in the tartan shirt, his bald head as red as a brick, was the one who had bought the house.

"And so you're going to just leave it as it is," Billy Kelly said.

"That's right. What else is there to do with it?" asked the man.

"And then what?"

"Then nothing. It'll fall down of its own accord. The place is half-rotten anyway."

"The word was you're going to build apartments."

"Mebbe," the man said. "Only, I've better uses for my money."

"I thought you'd brought me out about a painting job."

"I did," the bald man said. "But not up here. I've a few ideas about the lodge down by the front gate."

The lodge was so much part of Riverview that we didn't even see it when we passed it by. It had been unoccupied for years and years and was falling down. I had no idea when the last person had lived there. I don't think anyone had been inside it since the day our family moved in.

"Are you putting it up for sale?" Billy asked.

The man clapped him on the shoulder. "Sure isn't everything up for sale."

I hung out over the sill, thinking that if I had Beth with me we'd drop spit balls on their heads.

Billy nodded. "You might as well."

Then the man said, "Mind you I got this place cheap, that's why I can afford to leave it idle until things improve. Henry Cleeve has no business head on him at all. He's a bit of an eejit."

"Woman trouble," Billy said. "The wife was a right nutter. Did herself in years ago. He keeps a woman in Dublin these days."

"Mebbe I could have beaten him down a bit more so if I'd tried," the man scratched the ground with his shoe.

"Sure he'd have had to take anything," Billy said. "He got cleaned out like half the town by Nat Page."

"Christ!" said the man. "There's one born every minute. Mind you, I looked at the Page house as well. She won't be able to get rid of it easy. It has no back entrance."

Billy puffed out his chest, "You know what the problem is with Henry Cleeve? He turned his back on his own. He has a sister-in-law ruling the roost here while he goes gallivanting, and she's as black a Protestant as you'd find anywhere in the six counties never mind down South. Not that I'm bigoted."

I remained frozen at my listening post hoping desperately that God would strike Billy Kelly dead. I remembered the way he was always trying to scrounge money. And how he'd got me into trouble over the teapot. And the way he went on about things like the Bible-study group. Even so, I thought he was on our side. I thought he liked us.

When the men had moved away, up to the back gate, I climbed up to the top landing and looked out of the front window in my bedroom. The strange man's big silver car was parked at the top of the drive. They'd be back in a while to collect it. I intended to keep out of sight until they'd gone. I tiptoed downstairs and found Dusty with his nose pressed against the back door, his body quivering. If I let him out he'd go after them like a dervish. I caught him by the collar and tugged him after me, up the stairs to Auntie Theo's room.

I sat on the ground, resting my back against the bed, Dusty crouching beside me. While the men were there I'd forgotten about being hungry. Now I realised I was starving but I wasn't going to find much up here to satisfy my appetite. And I was thirsty. Good thing I remembered Daddy's warning about tap water, otherwise I'd be found dead from typhoid when someone eventually remembered to look for me. Or maybe, by that time I'd have been eaten by Dusty, like that old woman with the German shepherd dog. They'd come bursting in, Alice, Lynda, Josh, Daddy tearing his hair out, and find nothing but bones.

I poked around and found an old peppermint with the paper stuck to it, two cigarettes in a gold-coloured packet and a nearly empty bottle of whiskey wrapped up in a raggedy old sweater.

Josh once, for a dare, ate a cigarette. We'd been to a circus, and a man did a trick in which he ate a whole packet of them. The only time I'd ever smoked was in Page's, when Beth found some her mother had mislaid. I was sick immediately afterwards, in the loft, and had to pretend I'd picked some green apples from their tree.

I took one of the cigarettes out of the packet, peeled off the paper and placed it on my tongue. It was bitter and nasty and made me remember what it was like to have Auntie Theo standing right beside me. To shake the recollection from my mind I crept past the overturned wardrobe over to the wall, squatted there leaning forward on my hands while Dusty wagged his tail. Then I placed my head on the floor, bent my body at the hips and arched my body up into a headstand. I hadn't done one for ages. For a while Beth and I did them every day and also walked on our hands. Soon I got so good that I could walk across my bedroom. I could walk across Page's loft. I felt the rough wood against my hands and my hair sweeping off the dusty boards. Beth was probably walking along some bright sandy beach at this moment, one hand after the other. Her seat in the classroom gaped like a missing tooth. When someone asked me why I hadn't been at her farewell sleepover I said I'd been on a trip to Dublin.

Dusty had started snuffling around as if there was a rat or something. I didn't feel like waiting to find out. I called him to heel and together we crept up to Josh's room. When I went in I realised how much I missed him already. All he'd said going out the door was, "Seeya sometime Fran." He was the sort of person that hated fuss and goodbyes.

The cupboard door hung open and there was nothing inside but wire hangers. The shelves were tidy. The sheets had been taken off the bed. My brother! I went over and traced out his name in the dust on the emptied shelf. He must have sold off all his tapes and records. He'd never come back. I peeked in the chest of drawers and the dressing table for something that would bring him close. All I found were dried out biros, some old sticking plasters, a book of corny jokes, odds and ends.

I opened the small cupboard under his washbasin. Inside there was a matchbook with the name of a local hotel on the cover, a penknife and a round tin. Inside the tin was a lump of dried out dung. But of course it wasn't dung. I knew what it was. I knew what Josh did when he was bored or wanted to chill out. I'd walked in on him smoking the stuff. I thought it was disgusting, but suddenly I didn't care. I was going to damn well smoke some myself even if it did turn my brains into mush.

I managed to poke the tobacco out of the second cigarette in the packet from Auntie Theo's room by using a small piece of wire. Then, taking extreme care, I filled it with shavings from Josh's stash.

I'd never done it before. My heart thumped with excitement. I wished Beth and I were still friends and sharing the adventure. Maybe I'd turn into superwoman, or find out the secret of the universe. As I lit up Dusty moved away from me and hid under the bed in his usual cowardly way.

At first the homemade cigarette tasted disgusting but after a while I didn't notice because my mind started whirling and telling me all kinds of things. The light outside seemed stronger and the silence in the house disappeared and I heard laughter from hidden people. I stood up and tried to pick my way across the carpet to the door to join them but there were numerous obstacles blocking my way. A large python writhed in a distant corner. I tried to remember how Josh had done that tuning fork trick but the details kept evaporating. Plus there were dead people moving around on the landing.

Then I got very scared. I dropped the cigarette and put my hands over my ears to block out their hideous moans. After that everything turned very bright and full of wild colours and roaring voices. Men were talking to each other saying things like, "That's the youth today," and, "You'd never know what you'd find." Billy Kelly was saying, "All the family are mad," and "To look at her you'd think butter wouldn't melt in her mouth." Then there was nothing but blackness.

EATING CIGARETTES

Nat Page used to say. "If I was a woman I'd be a hoor in a high class hoor house."

I remembered his words as I made my way downstairs for breakfast. Not that there was anything disreputable about Myrna's hotel, it was a place for late-night drinkers more than anything else, but Nat kept popping into my mind like a Satanic messenger.

The revelries of the night before were finished. The place was dim, tidy, glasses polished, ash trays empty, the woman who'd been at reception when I arrived sat quietly with a newspaper.

It was Nat's idea of being a woman that suddenly caught my fancy. Women were able to hide themselves away and lick their wounds. Or go out and buy a new dress, or get a hairdo, or play the tease. They didn't have to make money. They didn't have to go out to work, they could stay indoors pottering and sighing over the unfairness of it all. They didn't have to be fathers or providers.

Then I thought of the scorn and derision Myrna would pour on my middle-aged musings. She worked her back off. She'd been running this place on her own ever since her aunt died. I was still unfamiliar with the details of her marriage except for the fact that it had taken place in Rome. Once I'd got over the shock of it I wasn't even sure that I cared one way or the other.

I sat down at a small glass-topped table and Julia, the cook, an elderly woman with the skin of an eighteen year old came through the swing doors from the kitchen.

"Ah – Mr. Cleeve," she said. I hadn't seen her yesterday. She finished work at 2.00 in the afternoon. "Well what do you think of the big news?" She moved over to stand in front of me, arms folded across her flowered apron, curiosity leaking from her faded eyes.

A clatter of dropped plates came from the kitchen and I jumped.

"Ah, there you are, it's your nerves," Julia said. "That's what it is. See, your nerves are gone and no wonder. I told Myrna you'd be fierce upset."

"Excuse me," I got up and made my way to the cigarette machine in the lobby, hoping she'd take the hint and leave me alone. The gold-wrapped Benson and Hedges packet slipped into my palm like a gold bar. I hadn't smoked for years. Just looking at Theo sucking at them was enough to put me off. But now I wanted one – right down to the soles of my feet.

"Got matches?" Julia asked when I returned.

I shook my head relieved when she uprooted herself to go and get some.

"I told her you'd want to know. I told her to write you a letter, not let you get upset and angry because she hadn't said a word." She returned, handed me the matches and pulled out a chair for herself. My breakfast was clearly the furthest thing from her mind as she leaned her plump elbows on the table and kept me imprisoned with her attention.

"Well, I'm not as upset as all that," I said. "I got a bit of a surprise, but I can still see that I'd no claim on her. In a way I'm inclined to laugh." I trotted out an unconvincing sample of hearty amusement.

"She didn't even wear white," Julia said, shaking her head. "Only a little navy suit. She looked like she was dressed up for a funeral, not a wedding. She showed me the outfit before she went off. I was very disappointed."

I had my first cigarette going. It tasted very strange after all the years of not touching them.

"A pretty white frock. That's what I told her she should wear," Julia mused.

"I'll have the full breakfast," I said, tapping ash into a glass ashtray.

"I hope she hasn't thrown herself away," Julia said, ignoring my order.

The nicotine made me cough. I didn't want to hear any more about Myrna and so I exaggerated the effect.

But Julia was unstoppable. "I've worked here for fifteen years," she said. "I could tell you things you wouldn't believe. That girl can get all sorts of cockeyed notions. I told her that I thought you were the man for her. I thought it was a shame the way she had you hoodwinked into thinking she was serious about you. And once she'd her mind made up to go ahead with the wedding in Rome I said she should ring you, as you were such a close friend, and tell you about it not leave you to find out afterwards."

I slouched in my chair, lighting a second cigarette from the first one, helpless in the face of Julia's confidentiality. She warmed to her theme. Myrna and her bridegroom had been going out for more than a year. In Julia's opinion he was the wrong choice. She was sure that Myrna would live to regret it.

"What's wrong about him?" I asked curious against my will.

There was a silence in which I heard the telephone ringing.

"Age." She leaned forward so that I could see the pinkness of her scalp under the ridges of iron-grey hair, then she paused and considered. After she'd settled back in her chair she explained that Myrna's bridegroom was an old man. Oh yes, much older than I was. I was only a young fellow in comparison. Apart from that, she suddenly became brisk and insistent about taking my order – there was nothing more she was prepared to say.

"You never know where you're talking, do you?" she said mysteriously.

By the time I reached Limerick I'd only three cigarettes left in the packet. I'd smoked while driving. I'd had two during a lunch break on the way down. Soon I'd be eating the things, the way Jane and I used to in the days when it was sophisticated. I could remember shared cigarettes after making love. A cut-glass ashtray sparkling on the lunch table. A cigarette passed from hand to hand in the cinema. A cigarette as we flopped on the back seat of my Rover car, another on a park bench, another after a ceremonious visit to her mother in the flat in Blackrock. I remembered packets circulating around the table as we sat drinking with the Pages and others in the newest hotel bar.

Nowadays it was easier not to smoke. The weed turned you into a leper. Also, in these hard-up times, the last thing I needed was to start indulging in unnecessary extravagance. As soon as I'd the house sorted out, and some sort of arrangements made for the future I'd stop. This was only a temporary lapse.

The last person I expected to see when I arrived at Riverview was Billy Kelly but there he was coming down the back path as I walked round of the side of the house beating off Dusty's rapturous welcome.

"I'm only checking up that the kid is alright," he said.

He carried a can of paint and I tried to remember if I'd asked him to do some work. I didn't think so.

"I'm busy across the way, painting a kitchen. I came over to see how Fran was. She was in a right state yesterday."

"What are you talking about?" I asked.

"The little youngest one. Fran."

I looked up involuntarily and saw that the curtains in Fran's room were pulled across. It was 3.00 in the afternoon. What was she doing in bed at this hour? I was going to have something to say about that.

It was warm and I suddenly felt as if my head had a steel band screwed tightly around my skull, which is the way I get when tension and stress build up. Maybe she was in bed because she was sulking. I thought of Winnie Page headed off to Spain and how Fran claimed she'd been invited to go and live with them; also her absurd demands that I let her travel to London. She'd just have to wait her turn. I was too shattered by the effects of Nat's treachery to get involved with such childish demands. Then there was the unpleasant surprise of Myrna's marriage.

"What dealings have you been having with Fran?" I asked Billy Kelly.

"I came here with the new owner yesterday and she was upstairs. There didn't seem to be anybody else around," he said. "We put her into bed and left her there. We didn't want to get her into any trouble." For once in his life he looked uneasy.

A dreadful suspicion crossed my mind. Who had put her into bed? What did he mean by bad shape? I thought of all the rumours and newspaper reports of murdered children, raped schoolgirls, abused innocence. Fear gripped me. I knew nothing about the man who'd bought the house except that he'd been in England for years.

"Stop beating about the bush. Come out with it. What exactly are you on about?" I asked. Fran had no business letting Billy, or anyone else into the house. A horrible thought crossed my mind. If he or the buyer had laid a finger on her I'd see they got jail.

"If you'd an eye in your head you'd have seen it coming. That young one was always on for trouble." Billy put the paint can down on the ground as if he feared he'd have to fend me off. "We didn't want to have anything to do with it, so we put her in her bedroom and left her to sleep it off. It's up to yourself to take it from there."

Sleeping it off was what drunkards did. I thought of a young girl left by herself and the drinks cupboard there to experiment with. I saw the two men walking in on her and tipsy Fran being spun some line, not realising they were sniffing around her like a pair of dogs.

"Whatever about the aunt being a right bitch, at least she keeps her in order," Billy said.

"What did you do to her?" I asked. "Tell me quick, before I flatten you."

"Do! She was taking drugs," Billy Kelly said. "And another thing I want to say is you'd better have that dog put down before you're brought to court. He took a bite the size of an apple out of your house buyer's leg. That man's the one who has reason to complain, not yourself, so watch who you pick a row with before you start pointing fingers at people."

I charged upstairs and discovered that the bird had flown. Fran's bed was rumpled but empty. I came back down to find Billy gone. I went back in and did a complete search of the house. I grew jittery as it became clear there was nobody but myself and the dog.

In the kitchen I sat on a stool trying to sort things out. On an impulse I went up to Theo's room. One reason was to look for cigarettes. I'd finished the Benson and Hedges and hoped I'd find some fags belonging to her. All I found were cigarette butts and a defunct lighter.

The room was a mess. Tomorrow I must fix the wardrobe in its corner against the wall. I stirred the tumbled contents on the floor with my shoe – clothes, a squashed felt hat, a handbag. Maybe Theo would want the bag in the hospital. As I picked it up the catch fell open. Inside there was a large amount of money and a bank book. I glanced at the columns of figures in the book and decided to give it a closer examination.

I'd switched on the kitchen radio for company. A soldier convicted of murder had been released from jail by the Brits. So what was new? The figures in their neat hand-written columns in Theo's bank book were. She wasn't rich, but neither was she a pauper. As things stood at the moment she was better off than I was.

The realisation made me feel marginally better about giving her the brush off. Judging by the dates of the lodgements a great many of them had been made while she was living under my roof. I could see her making economies in the household budget, cutting corners on the grocery bills, buying the cheapest meat, yesterday's cut-price bread, ordering less milk, screwing me for what she could get. I'd always given her whatever amount of money she requested for household expenses. If I'd been taken for a sucker and she'd been ripping me off for years it was probably my own fault but it meant that I owed her nothing now.

The question of Fran's whereabouts was more important. I needed to have a serious talk with her. Before that I had the sad matter of Dusty to attend to. I called the vet with a heavy heart .

"There's only one thing to be done," he said, offering no way out.

"Good dog. Good dog." I stood on the front porch, Dusty's lead in my hand, coaxing him and feeling like a murderer. He cocked his head to one side as if considering.

I walked towards the car, dangling the lead in front of him as I opened the back seat's door. He didn't need to be asked twice. With all the alacrity of a spring lamb he hurled himself in onto the dove-grey upholstery where he sat upright, looking down his doomed nose as haughtily as a French aristocrat being driven to the guillotine by a sweaty peasant.

When I came out of the vet's I headed straight for a newsagent's for cigarettes and matches although my hands were shaking so badly I didn't know how I was going to light up. On the way to the little shop I tossed the dog's lead into a public dustbin.

FLYING

When Beth was my friend we used to play a game called "Pigs can Fly." Whoever's turn it was – mine or hers – stood flapping our arms chanting, 'horses, swans, cuckoos, cows,' or anything else at all that came into our heads, '. . . can fly.' The trick was to make the other person flap their arms by mistake for something earthbound.

Swallows swooped through the evening air and Beth had flown to the swanky villa in the South of Spain with her mother. The herons flew down from the tall trees surrounding the convent and ate all the goldfish in our fountain and nobody noticed as I crept out of Riverview to hide myself away like someone with the Black Death. I'd felt as if had the plague ever since Billy Kelly and the man who'd bought Riverview barged into Josh's room and found me puffing away at the stuff I'd found in the tin.

"She doesn't know where she is," Billy kept saying to the man.

But I did. I knew perfectly well. I tried to tell him that I wasn't a sack of potatoes, and that the other man was holding my ankles so tightly it hurt as they lifted me onto my bed. Instead I said, "Lynda is having a baby."

They took no notice of me at all, except to pat me on the head.

"We don't want the boys in blue in on this," the man said to

Billy, and Billy put a finger against his nose and said, "I get you."

Next thing I knew they'd walked out and left me lying there.

I must have slept because when I woke up it was 6.00. I had to get up and go down to the bathroom. The big empty patch on the wall where the Mummy Madonna picture used to hang seemed bigger and barer than ever. The atmosphere in the house was gloomy. The doors opened onto empty rooms. I looked into Josh's. There was no sign of the tin or the stuff I'd smoked.. The air smelt a little sweet. It used to smell of Josh – the stuff he put on his hair, his socks, his sweaty track suits, of him. Even when he was out you knew exactly what it was like to have him standing beside you. It was an animal smell, almost like Dusty.

The tidiness of the room made me sad. He was always saying he'd tidy it tomorrow. Now it seemed that tomorrow had come and gone. The only traces of him were the little nicks in the door frame where he used to measure off my height when I was younger. Since he'd left I had started to realise how much I liked him – much more than I liked my sisters, even Lynda. Besides he was good at keeping secrets. You could trust him. He'd never told on me the time he'd seen me throwing Alice's good purple blouse into the fountain. Sometimes he'd written me notes for my teacher saying I'd been too sick to do my maths homework.

I couldn't help remembering all the fun times we'd had. The time he'd encouraged Beth and me to pick all the daffodils in Mrs Page's front garden and sell them door to door on the Ennis Road, for instance. Mr Page had told everyone the story. He seemed proud of our marketing skills. "They're only kids," he said to Mrs Page who was doing her nut.

Of course, Beth and I were finished. It seemed as if part of me had gone missing. She'd always been there. It was because of our mothers that we were such close friends. Mummy and Mrs Page became close when they were in hospital at the same time having us. Mrs Page once told me that they spent all their time sitting in each other's rooms because Mr Page and Daddy were too busy celebrating together in Jury's Hotel and Shannon Rowing Club to come and visit.

"You're mother was very tired, Fran," she said. "But I was worse. I'd never had a baby. I didn't even know how to put on a nappy. I didn't know that you had to sterilise a baby's bottle before you made up its feed. That's how bad I was. If it wasn't for your mother I don't know what would have become of Beth."

"Did she like me?" I asked.

Tears had welled up in Mrs Page's eyes. "Your mother loved all babies," she said. "She wouldn't have hurt one for all the tea in China."

She showed me some old photographs. Herself and Mr Page and my parents sitting at a table in a restaurant in Rome. "We were both pregnant the time we took that holiday," she said. My mother's eyes were closed and she wore a white lacy frock. I examined it closely, trying to imagine myself inside her. Daddy was holding up a glass and looking as if he was having a good time. They both looked quite young, especially my mother. Mrs Page was very fat and jolly with a scarf tied round her head and a sleeveless top that made her arms seem huge. Mr Page had his head turned away and you could see his bald spot.

"Did my mother ever talk about how she met Daddy?" I asked. I was hungry for tales of my parents and the world into which I'd been born. I knew they'd been happy once.

"I think she met him at a dance, or in the street, or something," Mrs Page said.

Her face got the uneasy look of somebody in a dentist's waiting room. I went down to the bathroom and then got into bed again. My stomach felt the way it felt the time I swallowed the ball of twine on the camping trip. Maybe it would get better if I ate something, but I'd gone off the idea of food. Just thinking of something as simple as toast made me want to throw up. I began to get scared. Maybe I was going to die.

It was like the time a few years ago when I became frightened of going to Mass in case I gagged on the host and committed some terrible act of sacrilege. If I did find myself, through inescapable circumstances, standing at the altar rails with my tongue out waiting for the wafer I'd have to keep it in my mouth until I got away to some safe place where I could dispose of it. But how would I get rid of it without crucifying Christ all over again? I'd had no idea and there was nobody around I could ask. Instead of going to church I started going down along the river bank and hiding among the trees to watch the seabirds fly close to the surface of the water in search of insects.

Sometimes people passed by, out for a morning stroll. Many of them looked strange – like tramps, or people who'd escaped from institutions. Some of them stood and stared into the waters of the river and didn't seem to be aware that I was there at all. I didn't mind them. I didn't care who appeared so long as it was not Auntie Theo.

Once I saw Josh there with another boy. They were acting very friendly, shoving each other around and laughing a lot. Then Josh looked over the other boy's shoulder and said, "Hey! Look who we have here." They were both out of breath and the other boy's bare chest was copper-coloured from being out of doors.

I let my head fall back on my pillows. Thinking was making me feel tired. I began to wish that anyone but Billy Kelly had found me. He'd tell everyone he met that I was a junkie. It would make an even better story than any he had about Auntie Theo's Bible-study group. I really loathed him, he made my flesh creep, especially because he'd smashed the teapot lid.

I seemed to have been lying in bed for hours. I'd probably be here for weeks before anyone bothered to come and find me, and then, with my luck it'd be Alice.

She had moved out but she called down some evenings while Mark was visiting his parents. Mark's mother, according to Alice, had started acting funny about her sharing a flat with him. She called to see it one evening and asked to go to the bathroom purely so that she could check whether there were two bedrooms and separate beds, as Mark had told her. After discovering the only bed in the place was a double one she'd announced that she didn't want Alice coming to her house anymore until they were married.

I'd been sitting in the room while she told Josh about this.

"Can I be bridesmaid?" I'd asked.

"Don't be so childish," she glanced at her watch, "I must fly. I promised Mark that I'd make spaghetti bolognaise."

When I had a love affair it was going to be tragic and interesting instead of all about bedrooms and spaghetti, unless I died right here, right now, which could easily happen.

I'd been sure Auntie Theo was dead. She'd be on crutches when they let her out of the hospital which would slow her up. She couldn't come flying at me with some kitchen utensil waving like a sword. But I was getting dopey. I could still feel the effects of the hash.

Making a huge effort, I rolled myself out of bed and shook myself properly awake.

Outside, I stood at one end of the tennis court and served all the balls I could find into the right hand court, then walked to the other end and served them into the left hand one. Dusty came and chased them and carried them across the grass where he crouched, waiting for me to prize them from between his teeth. It was one of the habits I always found annoying. But there was nobody else around so I let him run and snatch until he gave up and collapsed beside the fountain. I felt like giving up myself. I felt dire, desperate, filthy – I hadn't even taken a shower or washed my hair for at least ten days. It suddenly struck me that I should have gone to school today. I hadn't and nobody had even telephoned to find out why. I was turning into a non-person. My big mistake had been thinking the Pages would help me.

"Through thick and thin," Beth had said, but it was only her "thick and thin".

I lay on the grass, looking up at the sky and imagined that I'd turned into a crow and was flying over the trees and houses to perch on the roof of our loft. Peering through the gap in the slates I could see the two girls, heads close together, reading each others private diaries, or playing the "Love, Like, Hate" game.

I stood up again and swung my tennis racket round and round

in a full circle, and hurled it as hard as I could in the direction of the house. It was a good throw. The racket flew – more like a flying squirrel than a crow – over the railings on the balcony outside the little connecting room between the landing and Daddy's bedroom. It hit against the door but there was no sound of breaking glass. Dusty lifted his head and howled as if he knew exactly how I felt. I could see the handle poking out through the iron bars. Then, making my mind up quickly, I turned and headed up the back lane and out the gate.

FLYING

There was a gardening programme playing on the radio when I woke. Someone wanted to know how to rid their lawn of moss. My bedside alarm showed it was 10.15 in the morning. The lawn in Riverview had grown into a meadow. It was too far gone for the usual man with the scythe, it would have to be dug up and re-turfed. However, that wasn't the cause of my heavy heart. It wasn't my problem anymore. And Dusty was taken care of, although I'd rather not think about that last, forlorn, hopeless attempt he'd made to wag his tail. Animals can smell approaching death.

Blast it. I staggered out to the landing and knocked on Fran's door hoping that she'd make some sound, proof that she'd returned. I'd waited up last night, hoping, until sleep came in waves that threatened to make me fall off the sofa. Defeated I crawled upstairs.

I paused a moment, then looked into her room. Everything was as it had been the day before. The words of a song jingled in my head:

Oh, I could hide 'neath the wings of the bluebird as she sings . . .

But there was no Fran, no bluebird. Across the landing, Josh's room was equally deserted. The cupboard under his washbasin swung open. The tap dripped. A piece of sponge was placed under the spot where the drop landed to absorb the sound. A box of matches lay on the ragged pink mat. A bluebottle buzzed against the windowpane. I went downstairs. Usually the inside doors were locked by the last person home. Last night, in case Fran turned up, I'd left them open. Burglars were welcome to help themselves, not that there was much on offer.

I went into the kitchen, trying to decide what to do. What I needed more than anything was a cigarette, right away, but I'd have to go out for them. If I appeared in public in my present state they'd come after me with butterfly nets.

I felt like a sleepwalker. Maybe I'd wake up and find none of it was real – the children, Theo, Myrna figments of my imagination. There was just Jane and myself. The lucky pair – made for each other – Adam and Eve. *Tea for two and two for tea, you for me and . . .* I seemed to have a barrel organ in my head.

I boiled the kettle and dropped a teabag into a large yellow mug and carried it into the morning room. An envelope addressed to me with a London postmark lay beside the mantel clock. It was empty.

I remembered the telephone conversation with Fran before I headed for Dublin. Lynda and the expected baby had slipped from my mind due to Billy Kelly's thunderbolt, not to mention Myrna flying off to get married in Rome, not to mention Theo's mishap, not to mention the whole shebang. And Fran had wailed that she wanted to go to London then she'd hung up on me. Billy Kelly's story about finding her taking drugs began to take on a more sinister meaning. Maybe things were even worse than I feared. I saw her in the power of drug pushers. A young girl from a good family, gullible, lonely, she'd be a perfect target. The tabloids were full of such heart-wrenching sagas.

I groaned. The Limerick merchant who'd built this house in the early nineteenth century must have put a jinx on any subsequent inhabitants. Hadn't that been Jane's story – hadn't someone told her some nonsense at a coffee morning? The place was full of ghosts. The lady of the house had once tormented a housemaid who'd thrown herself into the Shannon. The maid's widowed mother had put a curse on the owners.

What would she say to me now if she returned from the dead?

"It feels like a prison."

That's what she'd said as I walked through the house ahead of her, flinging open doors right and left, opening up spacious vistas, pointing out the nineteenth-century corniced ceiling in the drawing room, the elegant proportions of the windows, the deep-shelved wall cupboards behind their panelled doors. When we'd reached the kitchen her eyes darted from the ancient Aga to the steps up to the annexe of the old-fashioned pantry.

"We'll never even use this," I said triumphantly.

"See!" I had the plans for the new kitchen furled in my hand. Workmen were starting on it immediately. The young painter, Billy Kelly, seemed to know what was wanted of him, so did the electrician and the plumber. "It'll be ready before we move in," I said as I shook out the plans to explain.

"So you've been hatching this for some time," she said.

"Maybe a couple of months. Nat told me last summer it was on the market privately."

"You looked at it even before Francesca was born and you never said?"

"Only from the outside. I didn't get to see the inside until . . ." I floundered, ". . . oh, a while ago."

"And you never wanted my opinion."

My heart fluttered unpleasantly. I thought of how she'd been since Fran was born. It had been a normal birth. I was assured that there was nothing to worry about. And yet, when I sat by her bed in the nursing home she lay with her fingers plucking the sheets and her mind a million miles away, not seeming to register my presence. I'd been anxious. It occurred to me that the episode in London was preying on her mind. Perhaps her present apathy was in some way connected. I planned to ask the doctor if she should see a specialist. My mind veered away from the word 'psychiatrist.' I had a dim notion that least said was soonest mended.

"It was all to be a lovely surprise," I said to Jane as she looked at me angrily.

She pulled her overcoat around her as if she was frozen and said heavily, "So I must put up with it whether I like it or not."

Women, I remember thinking helplessly. Give them the moon and they want the stars. Give them security and a beautiful home and they want some daring show-off on a flying trapeze.

"There's room for a tennis court," I said.

A smile actually flickered then died.

"Think of the children," I said. "Think of the fun they'll have here. Think of how lovely it will be for the baby to grow up in a house as good as this. Think of never having to haul anything up or down those dangerous front steps again."

"I like those steps," she said. "I like to sit on them and watch people walking past. It makes me feel that I belong."

"Sure," I said, getting angry. "And the draughts, and the cold in winter, and the fact that every time it freezes the plumbing breaks down."

"You could get it fixed up properly," she said.

I suddenly caught hold of her and kissed her. How ridiculous it was to quarrel about buying a mansion, especially when we were getting it at a bargain price.
"Nat Page did me a big favour by giving me the chance to buy this house," I said, lifting my mouth from hers.

She shook me off and staggered away from me. "I might have known. If he told you to jump off Sarsfield Bridge you'd do it."

I felt worn out. There was no point in arguing with her. "I've signed everything. I can't go back on it now," I said.

"I wish I'd never married you. You don't understand anything," she said.

I forced myself to act blind and deaf to her distress. If I gave in she'd make me as confused as herself. What I must do was make her come with me through the whole building while I showed her what plans I'd drawn up and painted her a picture of all the good times we had ahead of us.

I stood on the porch looking up through the branches of the copper beach. Pigeons cooed, swallows swooped and dived after insects, under the morning sun the tarmac on the tennis court seemed to tick.

At least the place was sold. It hadn't stuck on the market the way some big properties had recently. I sent thought waves into outer space, seeking Jane's vagrant spirit, wishing her back, asking her if she was satisfied now. I'd failed. I'd made a botch of everything. She'd been right. She hadn't married superman after all. Then I walked to the car full of forebodings.

THE HOUSE OF CARDS

After I fled from Riverview I hid in Page's loft. With everyone gone from the house there was nothing but acres of space and hours of silence but it was nicer here than in Riverview. It was bare and broken up but it was meant to be that way. I seemed to have carved out a place that was all my own.

I didn't know how long I could hold out in the loft. I'd brought some food in tins from Riverview and also a sleeping bag. We were having a bout of fine weather. The sky seen through the missing slates was cloudless azure in daytime and the colour of ink at night. But there were scratches and scuffles that sent my heart thumping. Most of the time I was in a lazy, vague mood. I'd forgotten my watch and so had to let the sun slice the time into night and day. I wished that I'd brought some books to read, or a pencil so that I could write poems. Instead I had to amuse myself by watching the antics of the birds. Swallows had nested in the roof and I knew it was late when they came swooping in like jet planes to settle for the night. Dawn was announced by their rivals, the chattering starlings.

Auntie Theo's broken hip must be nearly better. Soon she'd be out and about again. I didn't want to be around when she was released in case I was forced to live with her – I'd rather live with a vampire. I wished that she was dead and then became terrified by my own wickedness.

Over the years Beth and I had brought a number of useful items out and stored them in the loft. A handy red plastic torch was tucked away in one of the cubby holes that were in the top part of the building. On the first night, when I became scared, and the darkness seemed full of strange sounds, I switched it on and left it balanced on a brick. I must have fallen asleep, although I could have sworn that my eyes never closed, because when I looked at it next the bulb had become dim. The battery was almost used up. There were also a few candles, but I had no matches. I tried to remember the way to light a fire without matches, something to do with a magnifying glass and dried straw. There was plenty of dried straw in a heap in a small annexe. Wasn't there some way of cooking food if you had straw or hay packed into a wooden box? Exhausted, I fell asleep again.

Next time I woke up I had a strong feeling that my mother was watching over me. She wouldn't let anything terrible happen which was a comfort. But when I sat up my head began to whirl. I hadn't eaten anything since yesterday. The only money I had was £30 Daddy had left on the mantelpiece. I wondered if there was any money left lying around in Page's house. When Beth and I were little kids, her Daddy used to pull shillings out of our ears, and shake money out of his sleeves.

Sometimes it was hard to remember he was dead. I kept expecting him to appear like the time he chased Lynda in here for a kiss, and that time he went to the lavatory against the wall and we nearly choked trying not to laugh. When I remembered this I had to swing down to the ground and do some knee bends to keep myself from bawling.

I began to wonder if the burglar alarm was switched on in the house. If it was I'd set it off if I climbed in to look for money and the guards would come to check and I'd be caught. But Mrs Page would hardly switch it on if she wasn't going to be there.

If I'd had a camera the Sunday Mr Page chased Lynda in here and messed with her I could have taken photographs and blackmailed him. I could have given it to Daddy after he'd found that all his money had been taken and Mrs Page would have had to hand over whatever amount he asked for if she didn't want him to bring evidence into the editor of the Limerick Leader that her husband molested young girls.

I only had a vague idea of exactly what had happened to my father's money. But it was clearly Mr Page's fault. They probably owed us hundreds. Instead Beth had gone off to live like a swanky duchess in Spain. It wasn't fair. They hadn't been nice people at all. They'd only pretended to be kind and generous. And Daddy was the sort of person who was easily fooled. He even thought Auntie Theo was the right type of person to look after his children. No wonder Mr Page could swindle him.

I was beginning to feel really miserable and badly treated when a pigeon swooped into the loft and landed quite near me. We eyed each other. When it cocked its head I cocked mine. When it cooed I did the same thing. A favourite game I had with Beth was how we'd survive on a desert island. One of our chief foods would be wild birds. Pigeons were good. If I made a bow and arrow I could shoot this one. You never held a pigeon by its wings. You had to catch its feet between your fingers and cup its body in the palm of your hand using your thumb to cover the primary flight feathers as far as possible. But of course, if I shot it with my bow and arrow I'd be cooking it. I'd have to pluck off its feathers not protect them. As if it knew what I was thinking, the pigeon launched itself into a glide that sent it soaring out of the loft and back up into a horse-chestnut tree. I pulled a tissue paper and my comb out of my pocket and sat humming all the tunes I could remember.

I felt proud of how I'd cut myself off so completely. How soon would it be before there were posters with my picture on it stuck in shop windows and at the post office? How long would it be before I was given up for dead? I hadn't had a proper meal for nearly two days but I didn't feel hungry. That stuff of Josh's I'd smoked had taken away my appetite. Now that the effects had worn off I felt too uptight to care about food. I wondered if my face was looking gaunt from starvation. I had no mirror to check and the few windows were too covered in ivy and cobwebs to give any sort of reflection.

I supposed that Daddy was still up in Dublin with his woman. He clearly cared about her much more than about us. He hadn't actually said he was going to her but I'd known by his voice that he was. He always sounded smarmy and nervous and said things like, "You be a good girl now," or, "I'd love to come to the school concert but I just can't make it this time." Excuses, excuses. She must have something terribly wrong with her. She must be like a wicked stepmother, or else be really boring and stupid if he was afraid to bring her home. But no matter how bad she was she had to be nicer than Auntie Theo.

I dozed for a while and when I woke up it was still bright and I was ravenous. I could have gobbled up plates of watery stew or eaten whole loaves of stale bread.

I rooted through all my pockets as well as my knapsack. There was no chocolate, no biscuit, no packet of chewing gum. I would have to open one of my precious tins. It was then I discovered that I'd forgotten to bring a tin opener.

The creaks and squeaks of the night had evaporated under the morning sun. My biggest worry was of getting stung by a wasp. The garden was full of them. If I did get stung I'd have to go for antihistamine otherwise my arm or leg, depending on which got the sting, would swell up like a balloon because I was allergic to stings. If I got one on my tongue, here, by myself, I'd be dead within minutes.

I pictured the search party turning me onto my back and being shocked by my ugly swollen face. The poor girl. God help us all. Her father is distracted with grief.

I thought of Mr Page's face as he lay in his coffin. He looked the same as he always did. Neat, cunning, laughing up his sleeve. Maybe it had been an act and he wasn't dead at all, it was just a way of getting out of the country. I saw him with Beth on a golden strand. Beth had beads threaded in her hair and gold bracelets on her wrists and ankles like a little princess.

My biggest regret was that I hadn't brought Dusty with me. He'd be company. Without someone to talk to I felt as if I was sinking into quicksand. I poked around the loft, and found nothing but a single playing card. It was lying in a corner face downwards in a muddle of dust and pieces of grit. I turned it over. The nine of spades. My heart began to beat like a sledge hammer. That meant death. I didn't want to die. I didn't want to starve. Oh, please Mother of God protect me. Oh, I didn't care if the alarm was on. I was going to break into Page's house and find a tin opener and whatever else that might come in useful – a knife, matches, clean clothes, a proper pillow. And I needed more food than I'd brought with me. I was hungry enough to eat a horse.

THE HOUSE OF CARDS

Billy Kelly's story of drugs and the fact that Fran had gone missing made the situation seem very serious. I hadn't a notion as to what I should do. I pictured her lying hurt in some ditch or forest, or kidnapped by a sex fiend or a local drug gang, or murdered. The only person I could confide in was Alice, but she had no more idea of what was going on than I had and seemed more angered than upset by the news.

Anything could have happened, Alice said. I might as well know that Fran couldn't be trusted. She was way too secretive. Auntie Theo found her impossible, when she got a wild notion into her head nobody could talk her out of it. "She'll turn up, you'll see," she insisted. "This is just looking for notice".

I thought of Nat. "Softly, softly catchee monkey!" he'd say, except that it would be me he was talking about; "There's no such thing as a free lunch, Henry", "A man must pay for his education", "Never give a sucker an even break", "Maybe your little girl climbed through a playing card and vanished?".

He was able to step through a playing card himself. A late night drinking session in the Rowing Club: Nat takes a joker from the pack. He folds it in half lengthwise and cuts a slit across the crease leaving a narrow strip at each end. With it still folded he

179

cuts more slits at right angles to the first, from the fold almost to the edge, some more snipping and he pulls the ends apart and the narrow band of the carved up joker opens wide enough for him to step through it, pick up our bets and disappear out the door followed by curses and catcalls. He never cared what people thought. Nothing embarrassed him.

I was better off thinking about Nat than about Myrna. I caught myself hankering for her. I imagined her in white, twisty ribbons tumbling through her curly hair, her eyes shining for her bridegroom but in this fantasy I was the bridegroom.

"Don't even think about it, boy," Nat Page used to warn me. "It wouldn't be fair to those young children. She'd be entitled to the lion's share of all your property. That's the law."

It wasn't the children he'd been worrying about. It was Myrna spotting him as a crook. I could see it now when it was too late. If I hadn't listened to him I'd have married her.

I'd have brought her here to this house that was supposed to be Jane's house. Her warm flesh would have rekindled the cockles of my frozen heart. Her breath in my ear would have blown away the cruel things Jane had said in those last weeks.

I began to panic. I mustn't let Jane be usurped. If I did my life would make no sense at all. Besides this sort of fantasising wasn't going to help find someplace for us to lay our heads. Buying a property of any sort was out of the question until I'd put my financial affairs in order. I'd have to rent a place – but it was easier said than done. Even a three-bedroom, semi-d was way beyond my means. A boat, I thought. If I only had myself to consider I'd live on a boat. The idea had always appealed to me.

"Here we are!" I caught Jane's hand and pulled her after me along the path towards the harbour. I hoped she'd be as excited by my surprise as I was. I'd only known her for six weeks and it seemed as if my life until then had been spent searching for her.

A light wind rippled the waters of the Shannon. The small village was enveloped in a mid-week stupor. The nearest thing to human activity, apart from the two of us, was a bony hand creeping from behind a curtain. I put my arm around Jane as we walked down to where the boats were moored, made blissful by the way her body fitted so perfectly against mine.

She tilted back her head and looked up into the branches of the sycamore trees. A gust of wind sent some leaves whirling downwards and she pulled away from me squealing like a little girl as she tried to catch them. "Make a wish."
She uncurled her fingers and I looked at the crumpled scrap of russet red trembling on the gentle pinkness of her hand. "I've got my wish." I caught at her again, pulled her towards me and kissed her on the mouth. "I love you," I whispered then I nibbled her left earlobe.

As we continued on our way my heart began to race. I couldn't wait to show her the boat.

"There it is!" A few minutes later I stood teetering on the balls of my feet, not wanting to jump aboard before Jane.

"There's what!" she was clearly going to make a game of it.

"Our boat," I said. "We'll be able to live on it until we've enough money for a house."

"Is this a joke!"

"Why would it be a joke?"

The lake had always played a special part in my life: boyhood summer holidays, days out fishing, days exploring the islands and small harbours, trips to Holy Island and Dromineer. Sometimes managing to be taken on as a gillie to visiting Englishmen. The time I'd caught four pike in one day. Days with girls who were beautiful and sexy but were merely curtain raisers for the wonder that was Jane.

"Who knows, we might even sail around the world." I knew a man from the area who had done just that, on his own, in a small yacht. I'd helped him paint his cans of food with green paint to prevent them from rusting in the salt water.

"It's just," Jane gave me a sidelong look. "I'm not crazy about boats."

"Come on," I was in no mood to listen to her. My head was

full of the boat and the photograph its owner had sent me when I replied to his small newspaper advertisement.

We found the moorings easily but the craft I'd come to see bore no resemblance to its picture. He was obviously a photographer of some ability. He must have used a wide-angled lens. The thing didn't even look seaworthy. It sat on the water like a gipsy caravan put afloat; a hussy among sober crafts in tones of cream and dark blue or brown. It flaunted a coat of bright green and scarlet and was finished off with yellow window frames. All it needed was a fortune-teller's sign or a Popeye the sailor leaning on the rail to give the final touch of absurdity.

"Is this what we came to see?" Jane asked.

I studied it objectively. It looked as if it belonged in a carnival, or a playground. It was a child's boat. The sort of vessel I'd dreamed of when I was six or seven. Then the looped lacy curtains of its two-berthed cabin caught my eye and I thought, oh yes indeed. Why not?

"Now that we're here we might as well look it over," I said, trying to sound nonchalant. A blackbird warbled from a bush as if approving of my lustful thoughts. And Jane didn't seem scornful, only bewildered.

"They told me I'd get the key from the man who owns the shop," I said.

Jane ducked her head but I could see the dimples appearing at the corners of her delicious mouth.

"OK?" I asked and didn't wait for an answer, but ran back up to the street only to find that the slob who owned the shop had gone away leaving his premises shuttered and padlocked.

"To his sisters," said the dozy creature who answered my hammering on the door of the house next-door. I cursed all sisters as I retraced my steps empty handed, on fire with passion.

Jane had climbed on board.

"It's like a Noah's ark," she called to me as I came alongside.

I looked up at her, she'd taken off her sandals and held them in her hand. It was a poxy vessel, but with her aboard it seemed as bright and jolly as the good ship "Lollipop".

"Come up and take a look," she said, reaching out her hand as I told her about the key. We crept around the outside deck peeping in through the windows at the cabins and the dinky-sized ship's wheel, some bedraggled plants, pots and pans, a broken clock, a ship's decanter, a yellowed newspaper, a life jacket hanging from a hook, a compendium of games, two fishing rods. Jane sighed deeply. "I hope you don't hate me for not liking it," she said.

She turned to face me and we stood looking at each other while the water slapped against the keel and everything seemed bright with happiness. Suddenly we were tugging at each others clothes, seeking out each others bodies, giving cries of surprise and pleasure, then groans, then a shriek from Jane as the boat lurched so that we were almost thrown overboard.

"You're terrible," she said, clinging onto me. "We almost drowned."

"No way," I smoothed her hair.

"It's a manky boat," she said with sudden severity.

"We could always buy a bigger one later on," I said.

She pressed a finger against the tip of my nose. "Hush, Henry. Don't even think about it, or if you do forget about me. I honestly don't like water."

I moved back from her. "Listen to me," I felt I was making the most important statement of my life, "I'd never make you do anything you didn't want to do. It was just a daydream. We'll do something else. We'll find a house."

"I wouldn't even mind a caravan," Jane said.

"Well I would."

We stared at each other in silence. I felt we were both making big decisions. Then she reached for my hand and turned it over and began to trace the lines on my palm with her finger.

"If we had a caravan I'd read peoples fortunes," she said. "Your life line is really long."

"What else?"

Her finger journeyed horizontally. "And your heart line is longer than your head line."

"What does that mean?"

Her eyes began to shine with merriment. "You're a sucker."

Then she leaped off the boat and I was chasing her up the road and into the small wood where there was only us and mother nature and all the rest of our lives ahead of us.

 **DOVES**

I'd forgotten about the envelope I'd found in Josh's drawer along with the corny joke book, old sticking plasters and so on. I'd shoved it into my jeans pocket and then I'd found the hash and forgotten all about everything else.

I sat on the floor of the loft holding the packet in my hand. When I lifted the flap I found that there was nothing in it except a few sweets. My head felt wired and heavy as if it was packed tight with steel wool. As well as this my ankle was sore because I'd twisted it climbing in the scullery window in Page's house.

I wanted my Daddy.

Page's house had been a waste of time. I hadn't found a tin opener or anything else useful. The only good thing was that I hadn't set off any burglar alarm. I looked up at the sun, it had only climbed a little way into the sky so it must still be early. I wished that I had something to do. My throat was dry from playing the paper and comb. Anyway, I didn't know anymore songs. Not like Josh, who knew millions.

I tried a poem. I had no pencil and paper so I had to do it in my head:

> *Lonely I sit 'neath the trees.*
> *Mother come and hold me please.*

That was stupid. A tear slid down to the corner of my mouth. I licked it away and it tasted salty. Shipwrecked sailors kept themselves alive by drinking their own wee-wee. Yuck! I remembered the outside tap beside the coalhouse. At least I could drink fresh water. I could pass a minute or two by getting some.

As I stepped out into the garden the long grass in a waste patch rustled and a brown rabbit appeared on the path, its ears standing straight up. When I moved it hopped off as quick as lightning, flashing goodbye with its bobtail.

Auntie Theo made rabbit pie. It tasted like sour mud. To make it worse Lynda told me that rabbits sometimes mated with cats. If I reminded myself of Auntie Theo's cooking I'd never feel hungry. I was the one who was always dragged back and made sit in front of the messy plate until despair forced me to swallow the mess.

I drank water from the yard tap out of my cupped hands and then I splashed my face and combed my hair. As I made my way back to the loft I noticed that there were berries on the gooseberry bushes and also in the strawberry beds. Later I'd poke round some more. There'd be onions and lettuces and I could see that there was stuff in the greenhouse. That cheered me up. I wouldn't starve to death.

Back in the loft I took the jack straws from the niche where Beth and I stored them. Jack's are as much fun to play on your own as with someone else. I crouched, holding them in my hand and made the first toss. I was good, they all landed safely on the back of my hand.

I'd begun to feel safe. I was even having fun. There'd been some bad patches during the night, especially when squeaking bats fluttered around in the darkness. I'd wrapped my head in my spare T-shirt to keep them from getting into my hair. Bat pie. That was definitely an Auntie Theo recipe.

But now it was daylight and everything was green and silver. The pigeon that had come into the loft yesterday showed up with a companion. When I looked closer I saw by their soft colours and the rings of black and white at their necks that they were doves. I thought of them as friends as they cocked their sharp black beaks and looked at me with their redcurrant eyes.

"I wouldn't eat you," I said. "I was only making that up. I'm a vegetarian."

They pecked around the floor as if nodding assent. One of them stabbed at the sweets in the envelope where I'd left it on the ground.

"Hey, that's mine."

I grabbed it back and they turned and zoomed out into the morning. I wondered if they were married and had babies waiting in some flat twiggy nest. I hoped they'd be back. They would protect me from the ghosts that were going to walk through the walls any minute now. I started feeling upset again. I stood up and hobbled around the floor of the loft several times, being careful to keep close to the walls in case a dodgy part collapsed in the centre under my weight. Every so often I shivered as I imagined spectral figures grazing my neck. My ankle was getting worse. If I took off my trainer it would swell up.

What was the worst thing that could happen to me?

Auntie Theo blocked my path. She was holding up her Sunday school teacher's Bible with its worn black cover.

When she opened it fire flared up from the pages. "You wicked girl, you know what's in store for you," she said.

I wondered if it was yet 9.00. If things were normal I'd be on my way to school. It was in Sister Mary Ryan's class that I'd learned to recognise doves. It was while I was still in primary school and the class was making its confirmation. It was just before Whitsuntide and Beth and I were in charge of making banners to decorate the pillars of the church on our Big Day. We made them with doves painted onto a green background.

"Doves, not pigeons," Sister Mary Ryan said and showed us the colours to use for their plumage and the way their necks had telltale rings.

"It's important to get it right," she said. "The dove is essential in confirmation. It symbolises the Holy Spirit which settles on each one of you as the bishop performs the sacrament.

I opened the envelope and looked at the white sweets. It seemed a good omen that bird shapes had been stamped on them. I studied them closely. They looked as if they might be doves. Until my confirmation I'd thought doves were white, like elephants. I supposed that these were peppermints. I couldn't imagine Josh eating anything else. I put one of them into my mouth expecting the sweet sour, thirst-quenching flavour of mint but it didn't taste of anything but the mustiness of the drawer in Josh's room. A flavour of disappointment that just sort of melted against my tongue like a fizzy drink going flat. Somehow I'd expected it to last longer and be full of goodness.

In a while I'd pick some fruit. My ankle throbbed away but the wire stuffing had been taken out of my head and I began to feel as if my skull was full of beating fairies' wings. I wondered if Dusty was missing me. I hoped Daddy remembered to feed him. I tried to remember if there was dog food in the outside press but my concentration was going to bits. I couldn't keep my thoughts fixed on anything. My mouth began to feel like sandpaper and my heart started hammering against my ribs like a wren in a cage.

I fixed my gaze on the dusty walls. I mustn't have had enough sleep. When I blinked pictures appeared – elephants, a juggler's cup holding a pyramid of balls, arrow heads, rolling hoops. Then light bulbs that began to shine brighter and brighter until the glare forced me to shut my eyes. I was absolutely whacked. Next time I opened my eyes everything was a jumble of colour and noise. I clapped my hands over my ears but I could still hear the racket as if fire alarms were jangling all over the place like all hell let loose.

I put another sweet into my mouth and swallowed it frantically. At least it was nourishment. I'd tucked the rest into my sleeping bag so that the birds wouldn't get them. As I took the second one out the £20 from Daddy's money attached itself to my fingers. I looked at it. There had been a question on a television quiz programme recently. You had to know who was pictured on an Irish £20. I tested myself – Brian Boru? DeValera? James Joyce? After making my choice I turned it over. The note rattled in my grip like a fan. There was no face on it at all. Instead there was a big key, like the ones that locked the doors of the rooms in

Riverview. Underneath the words said, Key to the Kindom. I let the note drop and it landed in the corner beside the nine of spades, the death card.

I became terrified. I didn't want to have these sinister things around any longer. They had to be thrown away. I snatched up the playing card, my face stiffening with dread. My mouth and throat felt scorched. But when I looked at the front of the card I discovered that the nine of spades had vanished. As I stared, trying to understand, a heart shape danced up and down under the capital K. The sorrowful king turned his head. I winced at the crown of thorns. He looked out of the card at me and winked one of his redcurrant eyes.

I shook from head to toe as I struggled back up through the garden. My breathing wheezed and although my mouth and throat were parched. Sweat ran off my body as if I was turning into liquid. I was never as glad to reach anything as that tap in the yard.

I turned it on and began to drink from my trembling hands, but the more I drank the faster the water seemed to pass from my inside to my outside and the more I craved to fill myself with it. At last I began to retain what I swallowed. It filled my belly and my brain. Amazingly I started to glow and expand like a soap bubble. My hands grew transparent. I could drink all the water in the River Shannon and still want more.

At last I paused to catch my breath. The trees and bushes were full of faces but they looked on me kindly. My friends the doves came fluttering over the shed roof and landed at my feet. I wanted to pick them up and put them on my shoulders, but as I bent to do so, to my inconsolable sorrow, they turned into two dingy plastic bags.

Feeling hurt to the core I grabbed a yard brush and chased them away. Then I needed to drink more water.

DOVES

I drove in pouring rain to the nearby town of Adare. I had been offered a place, via the auctioneer, rent-free for several months in return for some caretaking duties. The owner was going to France and would stay there until late October.

"It'll give you a breather," the auctioneer said, looking as if he needed a respite himself.

The proposal was not ideal but it was better than throwing myself at the feet of moneylenders. The contract for the sale of Riverview had been completed. Time was running out. Also, worryingly, there had been no word from Fran.

Alice, in her role as big sister, remained angry and briskly unconcerned.

"She's gone off in a sulk, Daddy. She knows Dusty has had to be put down. Look, she was there when the man got bitten. It's lucky he has been so decent about it. She doesn't want to have to admit that it was all her fault. She shouldn't have had the dog upstairs. She's staying in somebody's house and she's told them that we know she's there."

"She's only thirteen," I said.

"I was ten when Mummy . . ." Alice broke off.

We were in Jury's coffee dock and suddenly I needed a shot of whiskey in my coffee and cream.

The big snag about the house in Adare was that it was stuffed with furniture. Fat chairs and sofas, lopsided screens, vast cabinets, enormous tables, crops of stools and knickknacks, cupboards full of china, shelves full of battered paperbacks.

"Excuse me!" I repeated as I bumped into the owner once more while he led me on an obstacle race through the overcrowded rooms. There was no space here for essentials I'd saved from Riverview. I quailed at the cost of storage.

"And there's the garden," he pointed at various aspects of it through heavy veils of net curtain. "Also," he stepped daintily across to a sideboard groaning with silver and picked up a teapot. "When you have a spare minute I'd appreciate it if you'd give these a rub." He waved airily at the glittering display and gave me a full-frontal glimpse of his fluorescent teeth which were nearly as shiny.

"We'll see," I said vowing I'd put it all into a sack. I wasn't planning to play Jeeves to someone with pretentions of grandeur.

It continued to rain as I took a quick turn around the village. I'd agreed to move in three weeks time. Maybe it was better than sleeping in a bloody ditch, but only marginally. I was greeted by two people I knew who stared curiously as I walked past the Dunraven Hotel. I'd be living in a gossip box when what I needed was the shelter of a cave. I ducked into a café where the cheese in my sandwich was straight out of the refrigerator and as tasteless as plastic. Leaving most of it behind me I headed over to the parish church. I'd done a job here years ago in a time when my days had been full of churches, schools, community halls, gardai barracks, hospitals – you name it, I'd worked on it. I wasn't yet 60, I thought. Where had everything gone?

I walked round to the dovecote at the back of the church in

search of some tranquillity. Columbarium, the old name for it rolled off my tongue conjuring up reverberations of sweet birdcalls on a summer's day.

Columbarium, a Franciscan priest in Athlone had given me the name. His sandaled feet plopped along the stone floors between the arches. I'd travelled from there straight to the town of Tipperary to give advice to the army who were demolishing a barracks. Now all I had were the ruins of my past. I felt a pang of self-pity.

Columbarium. Behind the church in Adare no doves were visible, only some chattering sparrows and a glossy jackdaw with eyes as crafty as Nat's.

"Give me your money, Henry, and I'll double it in jig time."

I banged my fist on the cold stone columbarium wall and cursed Nat Page and all belonging to him.

I'd been here once before, with Jane. Now I was alone and desperate with nobody at all to console me. I'd done my best. Hand on my heart. I could have disappeared the way she did, sought refuge with the winos sitting in shop doorways, or gathering on the grass triangle outside our front gate only pausing in their merrymaking to wave their meths bottles at passing traffic. For the first time in my life I recognised the honesty of their existence. They were the ones who'd seen through the charade.

Even my son Josh was wiser than I was. "You don't have to look like that, the money's not important," he'd said a few short years ago. He'd just left school. I mean, dropped out of his own accord. He was only eighteen.

"What are you going to do with the rest of your life – live on the dole?" I'd asked.

"I was only wasting my time there," he said, "Besides, I have a job already."

Once, out of curiosity, I visited a night club where he supplemented the pittance the local radio station was paying him.

Standing in the shadows I watched across the gyrating heads at Josh, weaving spells in a world all his own. Flicking switches, adjusting sounds, making wheels of colour and showers of starlight change the drab surroundings into a bouncing dream world. At one stage, to wild applause, he got up and strode to the front of his tiny platform and raised his fingers in a gesture. "Peace," they all began to shriek returning the salute and then kissing and hugging each other in a frenzy of youthful energy.

He had managed to spot me in my corner and turned his spread fingers in my direction. "Peace." I saw his lips mouth the word as I got up and slipped from the party before I succumbed to heat stroke.

I hunched into my jacket and paced my way around the circular building. The opening through which the birds could come and go as they pleased was in the roof. The internal walls were lined with niches on which they could nest and sleep. A door at ground level gave entrance to the monks who brought in food.

"Fattening them up so that they could kill and eat them," said Jane over my shoulder.

It was soon after we'd moved into Riverview. We'd driven out to buy furniture from a local antique dealer. Within the past hour we'd acquired a large pedestal table, the big bookcase, and the dining-room suite. The stuff was old enough to have belonged to her wicked ancestor.

I'd done most of the choosing. Jane hung her head over display cabinets crammed with knickknacks.

"Anything there you'd like?" I asked.

She shrugged and said. "Let's get out now that you've bought the stuff."

"They knew how to build in those days," I said to her, pointing out a tricky piece of masonry.

"You know what it is, Henry? It's a big trap." She tilted her head back and stared up at the top.

"It's a work of great skill," I said.

"It's a prison."

"It's an example of an old tradition."

"It's a one-way ticket for the poor doves."

"Get real. Come down out of that ivory tower," I said in sudden exasperation. Over recent weeks a situation had arisen in which if I said "black" Jane automatically said "white".

"Look," she said, "There's only one way for you and that's your way."

"Aw, come on," I protested. I didn't want to get tied up in a silly game.

"Everything I do is for you," I said. "What more do you want?"

She had the grace to say, "I'm sorry, Henry."

And, as happened so often at the time, her dejection cut me to the quick.

METAMORPHOSIS

I crouched, wriggling my face into grins and grimaces while I waited for the doves to resurrect themselves and come to me again. My lower lip bled where one of my new pointed incisors pierced it. I pressed my finger against them checking to see if they were still growing.

The trouble started when I fell on my face. I'd lifted my head, tasted blood and my eye teeth began to turn into a monster's. I brushed away a tear with a furry paw. My pointy incisors meant I couldn't close my mouth properly. I crawled over, dipped my head in the bucket I'd filled with tap water and lapped it up. It did nothing for my craving thirst. Then I started moving my face muscles to keep my teeth from growing even longer.

Everyone was going to be very sorry when they found me dead. They'd start screaming and bawling and shaking their fists at the sky. Beth would want to fly home for the funeral. She'd cry herself sick the whole way over on the aeroplane. I saw her in the black outfit she'd worn when her father died. She'd cry so much that she'd have snot coming out of her nose, and her eyes would look like rabbity pink pastilles.

She'd rush up to her bedroom where we'd spent so many

happy hours of our childhood and all she'd find would be emptiness and an old sweatshirt forgotten on a radiator.

Auntie Theo would be sorry for all the times she'd been horrible to me during my short life. I gulped some more water. There were two of Josh's sweets left. I was saving them. They weren't very nice, but I was too tired to pick fruit. Later, when I got a surge of energy I'd pick a barrel full. A large black spider came out of a crack in the wall. It was furry enough to be a tarantula. Beth was scared of spiders. I didn't mind them. Rats were my pet hate.

Pet hate – that sounded funny, like something you kept in a tank or a hutch.

When they found me they'd want to chain me up. The thought made me go for the water bucket. I splashed my muzzle into the smooth surface and drank once more. I hoped I was going to die soon. Werewolves reverted to their human shape as soon as they were dead. I eased myself back onto my haunches. The only person who would understand what had happened to me was my mother.

Animals can't cry. That's another tragic thing about them. I could feel the tears gathering like a black cloud inside my head, but the sorrow just got denser and blacker, darker and stronger, and shone out of my eyes they way it shines in the eyes of the monkeys in the zoo. Not a tear fell. Once we'd gone on a school outing to the zoo and for weeks afterwards my nightmares were full of glistening black eyes and misery.

My mother knew about that. She must have walked through our house sniffing the humans, knowing they'd want her blood, knowing there was only one way to escape. A clove hitch was the proper sort of knot to tie. We'd practiced it the time we went on the camping trip and I swallowed the string. That had been the beginning of my worst troubles.

I had to stay here until somebody came. It was the only safe place. If I appeared in the street I'd be hunted down and shot. And, even though it had started to rain it was summer and therefore warm. I wouldn't freeze to death like those explorers at the South Pole – or was it the North? Both, maybe. I'd curl up like Laika, that Russian doggie, years ago, they sent up into space. She'd slept into death. Beth and I cried when we discovered what had happened to her. If they'd done that to Dusty I'd never have forgiven them.

My jeans and panties were damp. I must have forgotten to go to the toilet. I'd thought Beth would have left some clothes behind but all her cupboards were bare. Not a stitch except for one grubby sweatshirt thrown on the radiator. I'd checked when I went inside. All my life it had been my second home. When I went in on my own I found a house that nobody lived in. The curtains were pulled across so the rooms seemed to be underwater. The furniture was covered with sheets like statues in church on Good Friday. There were no photographs anywhere. The Aga in the kitchen was stone cold. In the bedrooms duvets were turned back on bare mattresses. It was as if aliens had arrived and sucked out all the human life – or vampires, or werewolves.

I looked at my hand and saw that the fur had moulted away leaving bare skin and my claws had shrunk back into fingernails. Even my eye teeth, when I touched them with my tongue, didn't feel so sharp and I was able to stand upright and walk around the loft, waddling a little because of my soggy pants. I was still very thirsty and weary to the marrow of my bones but there was water left in the bucket. My energy was coming back so I could go and pick gooseberries, but before I did so I'd take one of Josh's sweets.

A whirr of wings heralded the ring doves arriving through the doorway and I laughed out loud because it was such a good omen. I felt that they were telling me not to worry and that my mother was close by. I went over to the sleeping bag, took out the sweets and popped the second last one into my mouth.

"Mrs Page!"

It was melting on my tongue as I heard the voice.

"Mrs Page. Mrs Page. Excuse me missus, is that you down there?"

The doves took no notice, they'd started their pecking around the floor again. I could hear the sound of heavy boots crunching along. They were coming this way. I knelt down and very swiftly drank a large amount of water. I was getting that dried out feeling again. The sweet had turned into a mini-volcano exploding inside my head.

One of the doves came right up and I thought it was going to peck my hand. "Gotcha!" I pounced but missed. The bird was too fast. In seconds both of them had flown away and I rolled towards the centre of the loft.

The crash of timber seemed like forests falling. I held onto the edge of the gaping hole as the low-sized man carrying a plastic holder full of milk cartons came in. I crouched overhead watching him peer this way and that. My teeth were sharpening again, and my skin was being covered with fur. My claws must have made a scratching sound because he looked up right and saw me.

"Jesus Christ!" He gaped then held up a warning hand saying, "Whoa there. Whoa!"

I remembered the time Mr Page chased Lynda in here. I remembered him afterwards, mopping his face and gasping for breath. I did what I'd wanted to do then. I gathered myself together and sprang landing right on top of the man, bringing us both toppling to the ground.

METAMORPHOSIS

Theo was still in the hospital and no arrangements had been made about her future. I had one hundred and one more pressing matters on my mind. The hundred was getting everything shifted out of the house and ourselves moved to Adare. The one was Fran.

I was all shook up and falling asunder. Everything was in a state of metamorphosis.

The trouble with Fran wiped me out completely. I was totally flummoxed to learn she'd been dabbling in drugs. I'd hoped that Billy's story about the hash was just an example childish bravado gone wrong. Alice had persuaded me that by taking her absence coolly she'd show up in her own good time. I'd snatched at her straw of comfort.

"Then she'll have to do whatever she's told," she promised.

"Fran, what happened?" I asked her when she was brought home. I'd been warned that the milkman she'd attacked was claiming that she was a public menace and should be put in an institution.

"I got scared," she said. Then she said in a quavery voice, "Where's Dusty?"

"Fran," I said, "He bit that man who was buying the house

201

very badly. You've got to be realistic. You know what has to be done when that happens." I felt and sounded false.

"What?" Her expression was wary. Her hair was brushed back from her face and she looked weary and sick.

"He had to be put to sleep. I had no choice." I kept my voice gentle. It gave me no joy to see how closely she resembled Jane, high cheekbones, dark sweep of eyebrows, that gap in her teeth, as she gave a cry of astonished dismay.

"Oh no, Daddy!" She shook me by the arm. I was a murderer, a traitor, a pig.

I did my best to ward off her blows. She was confused. She had turned into a little savage. She needed every ounce of care and attention I could give her.

"The pace of rehabilitation is really up to the young person's family," the social worker who was handling her case told me.

She also said that Fran needed close supervision. She must not be allowed go into the bathroom and lock the door, she must not leave the house unaccompanied, someone should be with her while she was eating, watching television, sunbathing, going into town, doing her homework.

I called on Alice for help. She tried to get out of it by saying she had to live her own life. If Fran required that much attention she should be in some sort of residential care.

"I can't find any place that will take her in," I said.

I'd made enquiries. Fran would have to be a great deal worse than she was before getting a place in a supervised hostel. Although we had only a matter of days left before we had to get out of Riverview I took the precaution of unscrewing the bolts of the bathroom doors and hiding all the household keys in a small safe in my bedroom.

"I'm definitely not moving out to Adare," Alice warned. "I've got my own plans."

She'd found a job as a doctor's receptionist and she and Mark were making serious wedding arrangements. "I'm not going to let Fran ruin everything," she said. "Just because I didn't disappear the way Lynda and Josh did doesn't mean that I have to get stuck with minding her."

All I could do was nod and agree that it was my problem, not hers.

I made my own attempts to play the good parent with my troubled child. My attempts were pathetic. It was very clear that she saw through me.

"I met Billy Kelly down the road. He was asking for you."

"You and Alice should play a game of tennis."

"So, Fran, anything you'd like to do this evening?"

All my attempts to communicate got the same response. Fran remained perched on a stool, saying nothing, winding her legs around each other and twisting her fingers as if she was trying to tie them into knots. The gap-toothed smile that wrenched my heart had vanished. Her hair hung in greasy strings. Looking at her I felt increasingly helpless.

The bright summer evenings made the days endless. Once I went to the telephone and dialled Myrna's hotel. When her voice answered I hung up. "That's it now," I told myself as I poured a large whiskey and drank to my lost girl friend and wished her happiness, and hoped she didn't give the old codger she'd married heart failure before they'd had some good times.

I took an old bucket with its bottom missing, fixed it into the neck of a sack and attached the neck to the bucket with clothes pegs. It was a trick I'd seen a school caretaker use when he was faced with the task of clearing up the debris in a school playground after the kids had gone home. The rigid open neck made it easier to put in rubbish and when he needed a break he hung the bucket from a hook and pulled out his pipe and tobacco.

I moved through the house with my cunningly contrived gadget. It was Tuesday, 30th June. On Friday morning at 8.30 the removal men would be here to bring the stuff I was keeping into Mallow Street where I had my office. It was a last minute stroke of luck. The owner of the building had agreed to let me the damp basement rooms for a fraction of what the storage warehouse wanted.

I moved from room to room robbing the lonely house of its last bits of finery.

"Isn't it beautiful?" I'd said to Jane, proud as a peacock as I paraded my new acquisition for her admiring gaze. Rich flowery smells filled the night air. Spring was on its way with all its promise of bright blossoms and budding hopes.

"There's even a greenhouse – with grapes," I'd said.

The grapevine was long gone. Theo got rid of it during her first summer with us. Tomatoes were more practical when there were children to feed.

"There are redcurrants and raspberries," I'd said when Jane was not impressed with the promise of grapes.

"So what," she was scathing. "I'm not planning to make jam. I have too much to do as it is."

I made the plunge into Theo's room. The wardrobe was still upended. I didn't want the removal men to see this mess. I stared at the rumpled bedclothes, the wrinkled underwear lying about, the papers, tracts, hymnals, baskets stuffed with mending, an embroidered bag filled with magazines. An old picture of the Queen of England was stuck onto a corner of the dressing-table mirror. This was alien territory.

"She's not coming with us Daddy, say she's not coming with us."

It was Fran, behind me her face tense and white. I felt a glimmer of hope. At least she was speaking to me.

I didn't want Theo any more than she did. I thought of the close proximity we'd have to endure in Adare. I thought of all the pinching and scraping in the months that lay ahead. And the uncertainty – I'd have to work something out – but, other than faking my own death, what could I do?

"She's so cruel," Fran said.

"Come on Fran. I won't let her hurt you sweetie. Are'nt we pals?"

She looked at me uncertainly, then she said, "It wasn't Dusty's fault. It's just not fair."

"Life's not fair. You're big enough to understand that," I said.

She made no reply, but she looked bewildered rather than angry.

"Here," I reached out my hand and tweaked her nose, then stuck my thumb between my index and middle finger pretending that I'd pulled it off.

"See what I've got," I said.

It was a silly gesture, a reminder of the time when she would run to greet me, babbling all the latest news, whenever I came home.

"You used to get so cross and worried," I said. "Then I'd put it back on for you." I pressed my thumb against her face. "Guess what I found under the stairs," I said, "Your old playpen."

She rubbed her nose with the palm of her hand. "Oh Daddy you're so silly."

It was the first time in weeks she'd grinned but suddenly she did, from ear to ear. Then she stepped forward and, placing her hands on my shoulders, clutched me as if I was a rock she thought she could hold onto when the ship went down.

After a moment I gently disengaged myself.

"Here," I said. "Maybe you could do some of this work for a change." I indicated Theo's untidy room and my fancy rubbish collector. "We'll pile everything we can in here then take it outside and make a bonfire. We'll tell her it all got thrown out by mistake."

"Really!" Fran's face lit up like a child watching her own birthday cake.

"Go on, you do it." I shoved the contraption into her hands and smiled into her dancing conspiratorial eyes.

In my own bedroom the brass bed that Jane had slept in was

dismantled and propped against the wall. I packed a few essentials. When I walked over to the window I saw that Fran was busy pouring paraffin over a pile of Theo's belongings. Sometime later she threw a lighted spill of newspaper into the centre. Flames shot up in a satisfying way. I checked that it was all under control and that she was safe. Then I went back to Theo's room and pulled open the dressing-table drawer and took out her bank-book and all the loose cash.

Fran was mistaken. I wasn't a rock. I was a man of straw, the biggest fraud of all.

 **LEVITATION**

The bonfire was fun. It would have been more fun if I'd had someone to share it with the way we used to on May Eve. I could remember those late spring evenings with Alice, Lynda, Josh and their friends telling horror stories as we poked the blaze with steel rods or anything else we could find lying about. When there was nothing left of Auntie Theo's things but curls of cinder and smouldering scraps I went back into the house and discovered the envelope with my name on it on the pedestal table. Inside was a £100.00 in £20.00 notes folded in a piece of paper with "I'm sorry, Fran, but you're better off without me" printed on it. That was how I discovered that Daddy had walked out.

I felt very small. I felt as if I'd been beaten. I was sure that I was going to be completely alone for the rest of my life. Then a figure walked past the window and the doorbell rang. It was the woman who had been keeping a check on me ever since the episode with Josh's ecstasy pills. She was quite nice but very busy. She'd explained that I'd been a victim of water intoxication and that it made you do all sorts of peculiar things. She said she believed me when I said I'd thought the ecstasy pills were ordinary sweets. She said that I was lucky the milkman had come in search of Mrs Page because he'd broken my fall. It seems she'd forgotten to cancel the milk order and he'd discovered it piling up in their front porch when he'd called to get paid.

I raced to let the woman in then I turned and ran back towards the stairs. I was only half way up when I collapsed, sobbing, on one of the steps.

"In a year's time all this will feel like a bad dream," she said to me pressing her face against the banisters to get a closer look.

"I promise you. You'll hardly remember it, Fran. You're young. You're resilient. You have your whole life ahead of you. This is a time when you have to be positive."

"Where am I supposed to live?" I wept.

"Hasn't your father made some arrangements?"

"There's a place in Adare but I haven't even seen it."

She tut-tutted a bit at this.

"Is there a friend you could stay with tonight?" she asked.

This reminded me of how Beth had deserted me and I began to cry harder than ever. And when I thought of all Auntie Theo's stuff that I'd set fire to I started to shake.

"My aunt . . ." I began. "My aunt in the hospital."

It was a mistake. A nanosecond later the social worker was on the phone to St. John's. When she hung up she looked satisfied.

"There you are," she said. "Your aunt was merely waiting for your father to make the necessary arrangements. The sister in charge is happy to release her at my request. The ambulance is bringing her out. This does not mean that Auntie is perfectly recovered but she's not being sent home on a stretcher. She'll be sitting up in front with the driver. I wouldn't be surprised if she dances a jig when she sees you she'll be so happy."

She laughed uproariously.

Auntie Theo walked using a stick. Her shoulders were hunched and, amazingly, I was a head taller than she was. The first thing she did after the social worker had driven off was call me Jane.

"Jane, you should tidy yourself up. You look like a gipsy," she said.

"I'm not Jane," I said.

The quick look she gave me reminded me of the doves in the loft.

"Of course not. Jane was your mother," she said.

"That's right."

"She went away."

"She's dead! Auntie Theo."

After that, I brought her bags upstairs and put them in Lynda's room. I'd have to make some excuse, tell her that her own things had been packed up and that we'd get them out again tomorrow, or something. When I came down again she was standing where I'd left her in the morning room.

"Has that baby stopped crying?" she asked.

I said nothing and she added: "You must find it difficult managing when she's such a little crosspatch."

"Were there babies in the hospital, Auntie Theo?" I asked.

"Too many children," she said. "Three are enough for any woman. You hear that Francesca? You know what I'm talking about." She looked at me defiantly. "Of course if you'd married nice Stanley from the tennis club things would have been very different."

That's what Auntie Theo's stay in hospital had done for her.

My aunt's return was the end of my childhood. During the ensuing days she and I moved, not to the house in Adare, but into a gate-lodge owned by a Protestant school. We were given it to live in rent-free thanks to Sibyl from the Bible-study group.

Sibyl was a member of the school board. She arrived to tell us we could have the lodge the day after Auntie Theo came out of hospital.

"Won't the school people mind?" I asked.

"Mind!" she cackled. "They mind my money, dear girl. They mind my generous donations."

Sibyl looked as if she was on her way to a fancy-dress party. She wore a large white woollen cape over an ankle-length green silk dress and a huge black hat shaped like an upturned bucket.

"So, little one," she cooed, "Your future is taken care of even if your Papa has gone missing. I remember when that girl – (she meant Auntie Theo) – came down to look after his poor motherless children he was out the door without a "thank you" or "goodbye" before she'd had time to say Jack Robinson. I fear the good man has a touch of the Houdini about him. I don't suppose he left a forwarding address."

I shook my head. In a way, I was glad. It meant I would just have to get on with things instead of waiting around to see what was going to happen. I just had to let things take care of themselves, I told myself. I was my own person now, and nobody else's.

There were never any ropes in our house, anywhere. The final boxes and crates of essential things that we took from Riverview were bound with miles and miles of sellotape instead of cord. It was amazing how, even when you thought you'd got rid of everything, there was still so much left. Dusty's feeding bowl which I kept in memory of him, garden tools, cups and saucers, bathroom stuff, a hoover, the kettle, a bag of toilet rolls, sheets, pillows, clothes, the radio, the television, floor rugs, a big packet of chocolate biscuits, the white elephant teapot. And I still had the ball of twine, or part of it, in my stomach but I accepted that it wasn't going to kill me.

Sybil oversaw our move. Alice hovered on the outskirts, watching.

We placed the white elephant teapot on the windowsill of the poky kitchen in the lodge and filled it with flowers that Sybil brought. Auntie Theo spent most of her time sitting staring into space.

"What's wrong with her?" I asked Sybil.

"There's an explanation, dear," she said but didn't give me one. Instead she offered to show me how the rope trick was done. Her solution went something like this:

Before the aunt and her small niece performed the trick they procured a strong cord woven out of human hair which was invisible to the naked eye. They attached this cord to the tops of two tall buildings. The aunt then caused her coil of rope to unwind and reach upwards. When it got as far as the cord it was held in place. After a crowd had gathered the aunt read a parable to them from her book of tricks while the niece shinned up the rope.

As the multitude listened enraptured to the tale the niece crawled along the invisible cord and hid in the shelter of the building. When the crowd remembered her she was out of sight.

For the next part the aunt, in a billowing cape, climbed the rope after the girl. At the top she produced a knife and started to stab the air around her. As she did so bloodied limbs tumbled out of nowhere onto the ground. When she was finished she climbed down, gathered the dismembered pieces of the girl and threw them into a wicker hamper. Just as she was about to close the lid the niece jumped out of the basket unharmed and, smiling, curtsied and accepted the rapturous applause of the relieved gathering.

"You see, child." – Sibyl loved to instruct – "The aunt had previously skinned and dismembered two rabbits and concealed them under her cloak. When she started stabbing the air she released the pieces and allowed them to tumble to the ground. We always see what our fears force us to see. The audience could only think of a young girl being cruelly dismembered. "Aaaagh!!" Sibyl's scrawny neck stretched into smoothness as she tilted her head back and imitated their wails.

"Meanwhile." She gave me a sharp look." "While the people were so distracted the niece crawled into the shelter of her Aunt's warm cloak, and back on the ground, while Auntie threw the bits of rabbit into the hamper, the little girl slipped in with them unobserved by all and sundry."

She looked at me again and said, "This story is rather in your line, isn't it?"

When I didn't reply she studied me then said in a soft voice,

"It's a shame for you to be so alone. Riverview should have been such a happy house. I once had cousins living there."

I remained silent.

"Watch, Francesca," she said, stretching her arms out wide so that I got the full benefit of her dazzling silk dress and the white cape hung from her shoulders like an angel's wings. Then before my eyes she floated gently off the ground, climbing upwards until she bumped of the ceiling and landed back down again with her velvet bucket pushed to the Kildare side of her head.

LEVITATION

I held my head in my hands, not wishing to look out of the window as the ground disappeared beneath me. My ears, as they always did when I flew, popped leaving me in a world of muffled noises. I'd cruised down the drive from Riverview, not switching on the car engine until I reached the gate. I'd left some money in an envelope for Fran.

Fran's attack on the milkman had been the end. I was out of my depth. Everything had become impossible. I could still feel the cold press of Dusty's nose against my palm while his eyes beseeched me as I hauled him into the vet. His doggy smell, accentuated by terror, still lingered in my nostrils. He'd known me for the traitor I was. It was because I'd left her on her own that Fran ran off to Page's loft. The place could have toppled in and buried her alive. Her attack on the milkman had been caused by terror when the floor gave way. His worst injuries had been caused by falling timber.

"She came at me like a wild cat," he kept reiterating, but I only half believed him. It was a scam to get compensation. The solicitor was a shady character with a dim office in a back street.

As the aeroplane straightened out and headed for England I hoped that somebody would see that my child was taken care of.

If I wasn't around they'd have to make some arrangements for her. While Fran was busy with the bonfire I'd made my way through the house. The acres of dusty carpets and empty scrubbed cupboards yawned in silent disinterest telling me to get lost. Most of the portable stuff had been packed into boxes except for a teapot on a high kitchen shelf and a few other odds and ends. The pedestal table remained in the morning room waiting to be dumped. The auctioneer had found traces of woodworm and refused to bring it into his showrooms with the other good heavy stuff the antique dealer hadn't wanted. I'd send a note from England telling him to give any money he got to Alice and Fran. I'd placed Fran's money carefully on the damaged table where she'd find it.

I'd be in England before the bank manager discovered that I'd left home. That made me feel better. And the staff in the Limerick office could sort things out for themselves. I'd done my best for them. I owed them nothing. Tomorrow if a big job walked in the door good luck to them and best wishes. The Adare house could be cancelled. It had been a bad idea in the first place.

I was relieved that there was nobody on the plane who knew me. Sitting next to me was a young woman with a bright curtain of hair caught back in a silver hoop and a shiny briefcase that she placed on her table as tenderly as if it held a newborn infant. It was not until she shrank back as I leaned across her to take a cup of coffee from the air-hostess that I became aware of my stubbly chin and crumpled jacket. I probably stank of sweat and bad breath. She was clearly unimpressed.

I'd met Jane on a journey. How many years ago was that? Fifteen, twenty – how old was Alice? 24 or thereabouts. Where had everything gone? I couldn't even remember the name of the girl I'd been involved with during that period. Initially I'd been irritated when the dark-haired stranger asked if the seat was vacant. The train was taking me to Dublin where I lived and worked at the time. I'd been at a meeting down the country. I planned to use the journey back to go over the notes I'd made and frame my proposal. It had been suggested to me by the client that I might like to take on the contract myself, use it as a means of launching my own practice. I had to use the trip to sort out the details so that I could concentrate on the gorgeous creature I was taking to the cinema that evening. I grinned to myself thinking of the way she trembled before I kissed her and moaned as my hand groped its way under her skirt.

The girl on the train produced a pack of cards and started to play solitaire. I shook out my sheaf of notes and tried to draw some valuable conclusions. After a while the alternating reds and blacks of the patience game started to poke their way into my dull lists of figures and pragmatic estimates. My evening date floated in and out of my head. I hadn't succeeded in going the whole way with her yet, but suddenly I felt lucky.

"The king should go there," I pointed out a move the girl opposite me had overlooked.

"Hey – great!" She gave me a blinding smile. I noticed that small parting between her front teeth. It softened the formal effect of her aquiline features. Then she scooped up the cards, boxed them and shuffled them and said, "I can tell fortunes. I'm very good."

I looked at her, admiring the dark glow of her hair, her shapely hands. She wore a bulky overcoat. I started imagining the body hidden beneath it. Growing intrigued, I put away my notes.

"You're going to meet someone new who will change your life." She showed me the Queen of Spades.

Her dark hair was heavy and twisted into a thick old-fashioned coil.

"Will she be blonde or brunette?" I asked. My blonde girlfriend had hair as bright and floppy as a giant chrysanthemum.

She didn't answer, but turned up the Jack of Clubs.

"You've sent a letter to someone and now there's no turning back," she said.

There she'd hit the nail on the head. I'd dropped my written notice into a box in the GPO in the early hours of the morning before going for the train. It would be on my boss's desk when I showed up for work tomorrow. I could have told him I was leaving. He was a decent sort. There'd been no need to put it on paper – but the dramatic finality of the gesture appealed to me. I planned to tell my date tonight and hope that it would make her see me in a sexy daredevil light.

"There are people who could bring you harm." Jane was poring over the Queen of Clubs.

"I'll take my chance." She was kind of seductive. If I hadn't already fixed to meet my girl I'd have asked her to let me see her home from the station.

"Tell me about yourself," I said.

She hesitated, then said, "I think I'd like to read my paper."

She put the cards back into her bag and unfurled the Evening Herald that lay, rolled tight as a baton, on the empty seat beside her.

I was free to return to my notes and my plans for an evening of passion, but suddenly I wanted my fellow traveller to pay attention to me. Did she ever wear her hair loose? Did she believe in love at first sight? Did she enjoy sex? Would she come to bed with me?

"Excuse me," she glanced up from the newsprint.

"Nothing," I said. "Just talking to myself."

"I thought . . ." she looked back at me again, then said urgently, "listen to this. It's awful. A bridegroom of fifteen days was eaten by a shark while swimming underwater with his bride. Fishermen tried to capture the monster fish. It escaped but regurgitated parts of the bridegroom's body."

I tried to make some sensible response but all I could think of were the gruesome details.

"I guess you shouldn't go swimming with sharks," I kept my voice light.

"It was his fate," Jane said very seriously.

"It couldn't happen here," I said.

"A man in Dublin was killed by a bear."

"But that was at the zoo."

During this exchange we'd started leaning closer and closer to each other across the table. My hand floated up of its own accord and stroked the skin behind her ear. Her hair felt even silkier than I had expected. I pulled her towards me and her lips were luscious and sun-kissed like fresh raspberries.

We leaned back and I saw myself swimming in her dark eyes.

"Where would you like to go?" I asked.

"Paris," she said.

"You need to visit Paris with a lover," I said.

She tilted her head to one side and studied me.

I felt myself floating an inch off the seat. If she hadn't stretched out her hand so that I could clasp it I'd have drifted off like a party balloon round the ceiling of the carriage. Outside the fields glided past interspersed with small towns and in front of me Jane grew more rapturously beautiful by the minute and my heart went into freefall.

HOW TO SAW YOUR MOTHER IN HALF

It was Sibyl who saved me. Riverview and my mother gradually became no more than shadows hovering as a background for my dreams. My father was a speck on the horizon. He sent a postcard with the Queen of England on the stamp. It was addressed to: Miss Francesa Cleeve, North Circular Road, Limerick, Ireland. The morning it plopped onto the mat I picked it up but before I could read the brief message its grubby edges became sharp steel blades that inflicted severe cuts on my thumb and forefinger. I rushed to the kitchen range and moaned over my wounds as I watched the skimpy message with "Daddy" scrawled at the end curl and crumble in the flame.

Auntie Theo and I settled down in the lodge. Hospital had knocked the stuffing out of her and no mistake. She didn't scare me anymore. Sometimes, in the night hours, she lost her head completely and howled that she was being pierced by a brute with a sword.

"Don't abandon me Jane," she'd wail, then whimper and clutch my nightie with twitchy fingers. At these times she always mistook me for my mother. Other than that she caused me little trouble and spent most of her time crouched in an armchair. Her chest had been damaged as well as her hip. Her breathing started to trouble her. Every day she grew a little more hunched and

219

small like a rabbit slowly suffocating while it waits for the conjuror to take it out of the hat.

It was a trancelike time with the two of us tucked away in the little house. Pine and fir trees swished outside, leaves lay like wet brown rags under the beeches. Holly bushes flashed scarlet berries in season. My sisters and brother were someplace that didn't include me. For all I knew they'd been abducted by aliens. Because of Sibyl with her unfathomable mines of knowledge and bright designs I didn't need them. All I had was Josh's tuning fork and the plastic cup and string which surfaced during the final move and were thrown on a shelf in my room. Someday I'd dump them. Their purpose had escaped me completely. All I could recall was something about sound and the Big Mover.

The only Big Mover in my life was Sibyl. She was amazing. With a wave of a wand she produced a man who brought his own tea in a billycan and painted the lodge inside and out in a single day, which was one in the eye for Billy Kelly. I told him when he stopped me on the road to call me a feckin' little turncoat.

"I wouldn't paint that black Protestant house if you got down on your knees to me," he said. "They've got you trapped, Fran. Godalmighty the sound of them screeching and singing would make any right Catholic turn in his grave."

"You've been spying." I stabbed a finger at him.

"Don't try to pull a fast one on me. I know what you are," he said as I gave him a look that would bend spoons.

It pleased me that his face turned puce and he clutched his chest as he hurried away from me, and stumbled like a man who suddenly finds himself at the edge of a trapdoor opening into hell with all the trimmings.

Nobody else complained about our hymn singing. We sang them at the beginning and end of the meetings. There was nothing secret about them, just an expression of good will. Nothing to ponder over, no sacrificial victims, no martyrs, bleeding hearts, stigmata, moving pictures, ecstasies, rosary beads or incense. Just simple tunes and heartfelt prayers. There was no reason to become baffled or fearful.

All the Bible-study group meetings were being held in our lodge. It was easier than trying to transport Auntie Theo to someone else's place. There was nothing radically wrong with her, Sibyl said. Just a slowing down, a gradual letting go.

"You mustn't mind about it, Francesca. It's God's plan for everyone. Today thou shalt be with me in Paradise."

I didn't mind at all.

We got ready for Christmas: red candles in heavy brass candlesticks brought round by Sibyl. Carols: *"Like silver lamps in a distant shrine,"* and *"See amid the winter's snow,"* and *"Good Christian men* (although we changed it to *"folk"*) *rejoice,"* and so on.

The man with the goat's beard and the older man with the surgical boot were still with us. As the weeks passed other people turned up. Soon it became so popular it was a bit of a squash, but that was a good sign.

We were back in ordinary time. "Are you saved, child?" Sybil puzzled me with the question. It sounded so natural and direct that I scarcely knew what to say. Instead I stood up. All around me the group pushed a little closer, hunched their shoulders, bent their heads and their whispered entreaties rose up like the rustling leaves new-grown on the beech tree's gnarled branches. Auntie Theo sat blank-faced in her chair.

Sybil leaned over me and touched my cheek. Immediately I felt my body grow as sweet and golden as if I'd been bathed in honey. My school uniform turned from navy serge to cobwebs of thistledown lace. And I felt that ball of string, that knot in my stomach, melt away. Sybil kissed my brow. It was a benediction that turned my heart into a glowing coal. I opened my mouth and words spilled out. In a short while the supplicants began to sing, *"God moves in a mysterious way/his wonders to perform."*

I heard my own voice soaring over everyone else's and knew what it was to be a prima donna. *"The bud may have a bitter taste/but sweet will be the flower. . ."* I swayed, all the lyrics in the world sounding in my head as I bloomed under Sibyl's loving gaze. If only Josh could hear his little tin-eared sister! It felt amazing.

After a while I lost the gift and needed to be saved again – and again. Every time I fell I was blown apart. I needed to gather up my scattered limbs and present them to Sibyl so that she could restore them, let me partake once more of grace and joy.

"This will pass. I promise you, Francesca. When you get to my age you know what you want. It is because you're a child you are frightened and astray," she'd say to console me.

I made myself believe her.

And then she was taken. We were in her house, just the pair of us. I'd done some shopping for her in the local shop. Sibyl was making toast on the open fire in her sitting room using a brass toasting fork, its handle topped by a cross-legged imp. Two of her patchwork cats, one mostly black, the other mostly white, blinked from cushioned armchairs. A photograph of a man, his head tilted back so that he seemed to be looking out from under his glasses, watched from the mantelpiece. His name was Digby. A long time ago he'd been her husband. I suddenly experienced an uncontrollable longing to preserve this moment forever. I wished I could always feel this way, safe and certain.

Sibyl turned to me as if she understood – and then it happened! The piece of toast dropped into the fire, the toasting fork with its imp clattered onto the tiled hearth. The two cats sprang from their cushions and arched their backs. Digby's photograph slid from the mantelpiece into Sibyl's grasp and tumbled with her onto the rug.

I was the one chosen to scatter her ashes from outside the boat club into the Shannon. It seemed right that a sudden gust of wind should blow some back into our faces. It seemed proper that when I looked up Billy Kelly was leaning over the balustrade. I felled him with my death-ray gaze.

I began to hope for miracles when I found that she hadn't left me. She was still Sibyl, still watching over me, making life bearable. Every room I entered I found her peeping through the window, encouraging me. What did she see? A skinny kid in leggings? A fledgling prophetess? Whatever she saw she looked on me with kindness. And, as time went on, she continued to save me from myself. And from Auntie Theo's distressing decline, from sneerers, charlatans and begrudgers. She made me brave. The time a fat letter came from Spain with Beth's address printed on the back of the envelope I dropped it, with Sibyl's approval, straight into Auntie Theo's slop bucket.

Occasionally, on one of my bad days, she steps aside and I see the dark-haired, tormented woman standing on a stool behind her. The noose is not yet around her neck. Her head is bent as she fiddles with the knot. She wears blood-red velvet slippers and her bare legs have veins and pink blotches. It's not the tortured expression on her face as she studies the rope or her poor legs that make me dismayed. It's the gap where her body should be. Instead of breasts, stomach, womb that bore me, there's a void.

It's then that I call out saying I'm sorry. It's then that I beg for forgiveness. I'm her little girl. I wouldn't hurt her for the world. "Besides," I weep, "Who'd look after us? What would Daddy do? It wouldn't be fair. You're my Mummy."

I rack my brains. "It's only a bad dream," I plead. Carefully I cajole and promise. I conjure up bones and blood, flesh and sinews, I restore her womb, I get Sibyl's bible and out sing Solomon.

"We have a little sister and she hath no breasts," I warble.

Someday I will succeed in making her whole again. And that day will be a good day, not a bad one. A born-again day all round. Whatever I did to her will be undone.

I see my father circling his car and beating his forehead. Mr Page wanted a piece of rope, now he wants to cut his tongue out.

223

When they notice me standing in the porch something in their faces makes me freeze, like a small animal caught in head lamps. Mr Page says: "Oh, oh, little pitchers have big ears."

Daddy steps forward, catches me under the arms and swings me up high, down between his legs, up, down, faster and faster. "Who's Daddy's best girl?" he asks.

"I am," I shriek as I fly back and forth, legs cutting the air.

He sets me back on my feet. Then he cries: "Tell me why she did it Nat? Every time I look at this mite I ask the same question. How am I going to manage?" But Mr Page has lifted the bonnet and is too busy staring into the engine to answer him.

THE LADY VANISHES

Jane's father was born in India. Ropes and vanishings were the stuff of the market place. His childhood was filled with wonders and enchantments. Ropes and disappearances were part of my past too. A young woman sailed for America and was never found again. Another ancestor was sentenced to swing for stealing to save his ailing wife and children from starvation. My mother stayed faithful to their memory.

She was outraged by my plans to marry Jane. "She's one of them so she is. That sort never change. All we got from them were the famine fields. Hell's not hot enough to hold them."

"That's ancient history," I said. "Things are different now. People are different."

She spurned my arguments as feeble and untrue.

After Jane died I made sure to keep well away from all belonging to me. There was nothing we could say to each other. Over the years, in the way that happens, people asked me if I was related to this person or that. Even if I was I fobbed them off with some noncommittal reply. It earned me a reputation for being distant, cold, a bit of a mystery man. Nat was the only person who had any inkling of my family background and for him such ties were best ignored.

"Who needs relations? I'm always telling Winnie she should send her oul' mother to the knacker's yard. All a man has is himself, Henry. Look after number one – that's my motto!"

Every so often he surfaces. Last time I came across him he was buying flowers from a curvy blonde at a flower stall in Covent Garden. After she'd handed over the yellow roses he snapped his fingers and a bank note appeared from behind her right ear. He rolled it up and tucked it into her cleavage. Then he vanished.

"Never seen nothink, mate?" The blonde gave me a filthy look. "Cat got your tongue?" she asked.

I still see Myrna clearly, short skirt, high heels with ankle straps, radiant as she waits for me to turn up and whisk her off to Connemara. I should have asked her to marry me while we were on that trip. I should have bought a ring and not that scrap of glitzy underwear. She'd snapped open the glove compartment looking for the map as we drove towards Knock. She must have seen the tiny gift package. She must have known it was meant for her, wondered if it was a ring. And then, in the basilica, I prayed but not for her. She was right for me. It would have worked out fine. Instead I let her slip through my fingers.

Jane has gone from me completely. There's nothing of her here in England. At weekends I sit alone over pints of bitter. I'm not waiting for anyone. Time moves on second by second. If I'm waiting for anything its for the moment when it stops.

A month ago the firm I work with sent me down to do a job in Windsor. It was as if I'd never been there before in my life. My room in the hotel was an empty box. The meal in the dining room tasted of nothing. I visited the waxworks. They looked the way I felt: Fixed, unchangeable, incapable of desire or regret.

I've removed myself from my children's lives. I think of them from afar, as if I've relocated to Mars. Once, in a pub, I saw Josh. He was on a panel on some TV show. The set was on a high corner shelf with the sound turned down. I stared over the heads of dart players as he opened and closed his mouth, threw up his hands, became part of the general animation. It reminded me of the time I saw Jane following the procession for the feast of the

Immaculate Conception. A clammy hand grasped my throat. I couldn't speak. We had no truck with each other. There was no contact that could be made. I hurried from the pub, unable to watch anymore, and walked through freezing streets until my brain was numb enough to endure the small silent apartment in Lancaster Gate.

I don't know if Theo's alive or dead, nor do I care. I guess the feeling is mutual. I still have her savings book but never cashed it in. I've never been that desperate. Someday, maybe, I'll post the book to Fran. It will be a plea for forgiveness, a feather floated across the widening gap.

Winnie Page, I feel in my bones, is still in Spain along with Mrs Quill and Beth. There's a moral in that someplace. "She who laughs last laughs best," seems to fit. Maybe Winnie convinced herself that the untold wealth was her due no matter where it came from. Probably she just followed some smart accountant's advice.

"Never give a sucker an even break." I can hear Nat saying it. I can hear Winnie's laugh as I lunch on my own in a wine bar off Fleet street. The counter is a narrow shelf. I perch, like a dunce on a stool, facing the wall.

Riverview rises up before me. I hear Nat: "It's all yours, boy. Thank your Uncle Nat." I reapply myself to my ham sandwich, take a sip of sour wine.

Now and again I glance at an Irish newspaper. The recession has ended. Everything, especially property prices, are rocketing skywards. An apartment block in Limerick called Riverview Close is sold at a new high off the architect's plans. "One of Limerick's most desirable locations" the article says.

"I don't want to think about it," I say to Nat as I face him across a restaurant with white tablecloths in Soho's Chinatown.

"This is the trick," he says, his face inscrutable. Then he shows me that I must rest the fat end of one stick in the saddle of my thumb and grip the lower part of it between my second and third fingers. Next I must grasp the other stick between the thumb and forefinger of the same hand, catching it halfway along its length. Next (he demonstrates) I articulate the tip of that stick against the lower one.

I stare fascinated by his deft, light fingers.

"Then you pinch the food, sir," the waitress murmurs in my ear.

Chinese people put their hands over their mouths and beg your pardon when they laugh. The people at the next table hold their bowls closer to their faces to conceal their amusement.

"Or you can shovel it up, or flick it in," Nat calls after me as I head for the cashier's desk, leaving my dish of rice and prawns for him to enjoy.

I must be a grandfather, maybe several times over. Who needs a granddad like me? The last baby I ever picked up was Fran. Jane sat staring out into the garden. The cigarette jiggled between her fingers.

"You change her," she said. Her voice was hard. "She's your child as much as mine."

"Ok," I humoured her. "But I'll have to take off my suit before I do."

The doctor had told me that she seemed to be suffering from a post-natal depression. It sometimes happened. The cause was chemical. It passed of its own accord. In the meantime I must be patient, bide my time. Moving house might be the very thing to bring her round, he said. I'd got myself a fine piece of property. Any woman would be happy to be mistress of such a gracious home.

"It feels like a prison."

Jane's remark came like a blow to the back of my head. Tears sprang to my eyes. I was overworked and under stress. My blood pressure was way, way up.

Feck it! I refused to believe she'd said such a stupid thing.

I entered the house without her. After a while she pattered in behind me. Her protests were pathetic. We faced each other in the decrepit kitchen and I beat down her objections with my roll of plans.

"So, it doesn't matter what I say," she stood back from me. Her face was very pale.

"Look at me," I said, pulling her into my arms.

"I am looking," she said.

"Well?"

"I'd rather live on that tub of a boat you once fancied buying." She clutched my shoulders. I could see she was fighting back tears.

"I'll buy you a boat as well," I said, then nibbled her earlobe. That day in Shannon Harbour came back to me. "And a caravan. You can park it out on the lawn and tell fortunes."

She jumped away from me as if she'd been stung.

"No thanks," she said. "There's nothing but grief ahead."

"You used to be good at it," I said. "After all you caught me by reading the cards."

She said nothing.

The house settled around us. I could feel it drawing us in. I knew exactly what I was going to do. All that plumbing would have to go. The old Aga belonged in a rubbish dump. And then there were the reception rooms, and the upstairs.

"Come on," I said to Jane. "I'll show you the rest of it."

"I'm not in the humour," she said.

I felt as if she'd turned into a stranger. Tiredness crept over me, dragging me down. I had to get out. I brushed past her and went and walked from room to room. She was still waiting when I returned about half an hour later. She looked so lost that I immediately felt remorseful. But it was too late. The spell was broken.

I didn't understand at the time, but looking back I see that I was the one who had been deceived by my own dreams. Jane needed time to adjust, get back on her feet. She was going through a crisis. She needed better medical attention, not surprise houses. When I ignored her objections she realised that the game was up. When I dismissed her real anxiety as a silly whim I destroyed her.

Gradually, over the next few months, she became monosyllabic and remote. I have no idea how she felt on that last morning. Some questions have no answers. Some secrets can never be divulged. Some lost people are never found. I accept the truth of this as I feel myself disappear without a trace in the wake of what has gone before.

End